WISH ON
A UNICORN

KAREN HESSE

SQUARE
FISH

HENRY HOLT AND COMPANY

For Kate and Rachel,
who have always believed in unicorns,
and for Randy,
who has always believed in me

SQUARE
FISH

An Imprint of Macmillan

WISH ON A UNICORN. Copyright © 1992 by Karen Hesse. All rights re-
served. Printed in the United States of America. For information, address
Square Fish, 175 Fifth Avenue, New York, N.Y. 10010.

Square Fish and the Square Fish logo are trademarks of Macmillan
and are used by Henry Holt and Company under license from Macmillan.

Library of Congress Cataloging-in-Publication Data
Hesse, Karen.
Wish on a unicorn / Karen Hesse.
Summary: Sixth-grader Maggie feels burdened by her seven-year-old
sister, Hannie, who is slightly brain-damaged and believes that a toy
unicorn has magical powers, until one afternoon a crisis shows her
how special Hannie is.
ISBN-13: 978-0-312-37611-6 / ISBN-10: 0-312-37611-1
[1. Sisters—Fiction.   2. Mentally handicapped—Fiction.
3. Wishes—Fiction.]   I. Title.
PZ7.H4364Wi   1991
[Fic]—dc20   90-5320

Originally published in the United States by Henry Holt and Company
Square Fish logo designed by Filomena Tuosto
First Square Fish Edition: March 2009
10 9 8 7 6 5 4 3 2 1
www.squarefishbooks.com

WISH ON
A UNICORN

1

Hannie and I were walking home from school when we saw a unicorn in Newell's field. It wasn't a real unicorn. There's no such thing as a real unicorn. It was just a stuffed thing, propped up against the fence post.

Hannie ran toward it, her chunky legs and arms flapping as she went, her short, dark hair flying every which way, but I wasn't moving my skinny self over there in any hurry. I'm the oldest, so I guess I know how to act, even though some folks think I don't. Well, I know a thing or two. And I sure know one of Brody Lawson's tricks before I get tied in a knot over it.

Brody wasn't going to see me run after some old

1

stuffed toy. I felt pretty sure he was out there, waiting and watching, looking for a chance to make my life miserable. Well, he'd be waiting a long time if I had anything to do with it.

Hannie circled round the unicorn, which was leaning against the fence in the long dry grass. It stood tall as Hannie's waist and was dingy white, like it'd been dragged through the dust and back again.

"It real?" Hannie asked, stroking its mane.

Hannie's different from other kids. She looks normal enough, except one eye is bigger than the other, but she talks baby talk, even if she is nearly eight, so only Mama and me and my little brother, Mooch, can figure what she's saying. Mama says Hannie's slow on account of she didn't get enough air to breathe when she was being born.

Hannie's slow all right. Mooch is almost two years younger, but he already knows more than Hannie does. He can even read a little. Hannie can't read her own name. All the other kids in her class can read some, but not Hannie.

Mama says I have to look out for Hannie and Mooch and teach them a thing or two about this world. Mama doesn't know what a tall order that can be sometimes. Kids at school, especially Patty Jo and Alice, they won't talk to me because of Hannie, even though sometimes I think Patty Jo wouldn't mind being friends. I guess they're afraid Hannie'll rub off on them or something.

"It real?" Hannie asked again.

"Course it's not real, Hannie," I said. "There's no such thing as a real unicorn. Unicorns are just something you read about in storybooks."

I could hear the traffic picking up on the highway behind us. Even on my best day I can't hear those cars and trucks ripping past without feeling spooked. The ground just shakes underneath me and my insides get to shaking too.

"Why it here?" Hannie asked. She was squatting in front of the unicorn.

I shrugged. "How should I know?"

Hannie picked leaves and dried grass off the unicorn. "Hannie take it home?"

"We can't take it, Hannie," I said. "It doesn't belong to us, and besides, Mama'd never let us keep it. It's too ratty."

"Not ratty," Hannie said. "Pretty!"

She really meant it too.

"Just look at it, Hannie," I said. "The unicorn's horn is drooping over and the head's hanging like somebody tried twisting it off. Mama won't even let it in the house."

"Mama might," Hannie said. "Mags ask."

Hannie's forever thinking I can do anything. Well, even if I can do most things, there are some things I cannot do, and one of those things is to talk Mama into keeping an old stuffed unicorn. I know Mama. She'd take one look at that old thing and toss it out faster than spoiled milk.

"Quit touching it, Hannie," I said. "You're getting yourself filthy."

She kept hugging it anyway. "Hannie's unicorn," she said.

"Come on. Leave it alone now. I'll race you home, Hannie. Loser clears dinner for a week."

Hannie runs slower than cold gravy, but I would've let her win just to get her away from that old unicorn.

Hannie squinted her good eye up at me. "Hannie not leave it, Mags."

Brakes squealed up on the highway behind us and someone laid on their horn.

"It's getting late, Hannie," I said, feeling my stomach going to jelly from being so close to the road. "We got to get back home."

"Hannie bring unicorn?"

"No!" I said. "We got to leave it here, Hannie. I'm sure it belongs to someone." I was thinking probably it belonged to old Brody Lawson. It'd be just like him to twist a unicorn's neck.

"Unicorn got magic, Mags," Hannie said.

"No, Hannie. That's just in stories. That's real good you remember what I read to you, but those are fairy tales, Hannie, make-believe. You got a stuffed unicorn there. It's not real. It can't ever be real. And it doesn't have one bit of magic in it."

"Does," Hannie insisted, shoving the dirty unicorn into my face. "Make wish, Mags."

"Wishes don't ever come true, Hannie. Especially not wishes made on a broken-down old unicorn. Believe me."

If wishes did come true, I sure wouldn't be standing on the edge of Newell's field with the highway ripping along behind me, waiting for my sister to make up her mind to go home. I know for a fact wishes definitely do not come true.

"Hannie not leave it."

"Come on, Hannie. We got to get home. Mooch is waiting and I've got chores and I still need to write that stupid essay for Mrs. Fribush."

Mrs. Fribush is my sixth-grade teacher. She assigned us this essay to write about our families. Shoot, I get embarrassed just thinking about my family, let alone writing about it.

"Let's go, Hannie," I said, squinting my eyes up like Mama does when she's losing her temper. "I really mean it this time."

Hannie sat down right in the long grass and refused to come.

I looked around, sure that Brody was watching from somewhere. That was just like Brody, to go sneaking around pretending he wasn't there and listening meanwhile to everything you said so he could throw it back in your face next time he had a good crowd. He surely must be behind this. Who else would be so sly-dog mean as to saddle me with a stuffed unicorn that my sister wouldn't let alone?

I scowled blacker than best shoes. Why do I always get stuck with Hannie?

"What are you going to tell Mama?" I asked. "She's never gonna let us bring this unicorn inside."

"Hide it, Mags," Hannie said. "See."

She stuck the filthy old unicorn behind her and it poked out umpty-dozen places from her back, but she was grinning so the freckles on her nose squinched up close against each other.

That Hannie's as stubborn as an elbow.

"All right," I said, helping her up. "Come on."

I'm not sure how she did it, but somehow Hannie'd sucked me into bringing that unicorn down the road to home.

2

We were almost to the trailer when Mooch banged out the door and raced down the road to meet us. He's just an inch or two shorter than Hannie and his eyes are both the same size, but other than that they look like two sides of the same door. They both have their daddy's dark hair and they both wear it the same. Mama puts the pancake bowl on their heads and cuts around the rim. Mooch and Hannie are my half-brother and -sister. We don't look anything alike. Me, I've got long blond hair, like Mama.

Me and Mama, we're just a pair of iced-tea spoons—long and skinny. I can't say if I look anything like my daddy. I wish I could. I wish I could remember my daddy, even a little, but I was only two when he died. I can't help wondering sometimes what he was like and how things might be if he was still around.

Mama won't talk about him. Not at all. When I used to ask Mama about Daddy, she'd get all closed up like she'd locked herself in a room. Not a real room. I could see her all right; I just couldn't get to her. She was seventeen when Daddy died. That's not very old. Some folks wanted to take me away from Mama; they said she couldn't take care of me. Mama showed them.

My daddy dying like that was hard on Mama, but it's hard on me, too. There's just some things I want to know, like what my daddy looked like and what he sounded like and what we did when we were all-together family.

All I know about my daddy is that he went up to the highway one night. He went up to the highway and there was an accident and he never came back.

When Hannie and Mooch's daddy lived with us, he was nice enough to me. But sometimes he was mean to Mama. Meaner than burning rubber. That was usually when he was drunk. One night he knocked Mama around and started coming for us kids. Mama threw him out. Skinny as she is, she pushed him right down the trailer steps and out onto the lawn. He banged at the trailer door for a long time and yelled and said he was sorry, but Mama wouldn't let him in. I started to get up, but Mama told me to just stay put. She climbed in bed with me and held me till things quieted down. In the morning he was gone.

Sometimes I miss him. When he was around, we felt like family. But Mama doesn't miss him, I know that for a fact, 'cause she's told me about a million times. She says even if she does have to work all hours of the day and night, she still don't miss that man any more than you'd miss a toothache.

"Ohhh," said Mooch, catching up to us and admiring the unicorn. "Where'd you get that?"

"Down there," Hannie said, pointing back toward Newell's field. "Make wish, Moochie. Magic wish."

Mooch took a solid step back and crossed his arms in front of him. "She making fun of me, Mags?"

I shook my head no.

"Really?" he asked, looking at me again. "I can make a wish on that old thing and it will come true?"

I shrugged. "Hannie's telling this story, Mooch."

"Well, if it's true," Mooch said, reaching out and

batting at the horn of the unicorn, "I wish I had something to eat."

It was just like Mooch to be thinking about food. He was always thinking about food. I dug my lunch bag out and tossed it to him.

Mooch tore into the bag and started ripping bites off the stale sandwich. "Mmm. Ffnks," he said.

"Quit talking with your mouth full, Mooch," I said. "It's not polite."

Mooch stuck his butt in my face, sassing me.

Someone has got to teach that boy a thing or two. He's already been in more trouble than most kids twice his age.

I had one foot on the first step of the trailer before I looked back and saw Hannie standing deer still in the middle of the road, staring at the unicorn.

"Moochie's wish," she said. "Moochie's wish."

I walked back to her. "You mean him wishing on the unicorn for something to eat? You think my leftover sandwich means his wish came true? You know I save him my sandwich every day, Hannie. You know that!"

I wouldn't be caught dead eating that stupid sandwich in front of Patty Jo and Alice. They come into the lunchroom with their little bitty containers of chicken and boxed pretzels, and grapes already picked off the branches and hard-boiled eggs with little saltshakers made out of cardboard that you throw away when you're done. And me with just two slices of white bread and jelly in the middle. Forget it. I'd rather starve than pull out that measly old lunch in front of them.

"Moochie's wish," Hannie kept repeating.

"You're talking nonsense," I said, leading the two of them out of the road and back toward the trailer. "That dirty old unicorn can't grant wishes any better than I can."

Hannie looked up at me with the dumbest old cow look on her face and dumped that unicorn into my arms. "Mags make wish."

"I'm not making any wishes," I said, holding the unicorn like it was a load of dirty shorts. "When you go wishing for things, all you get is disappointed."

If half the things I'd wished for had come true in the last couple years, I sure wouldn't need any old unicorn, magic or not. I'd be living in a real house, with pretty clothes that nobody ever wore before me, and so much good food I could invite Patty Jo and Alice over seven days a week and we'd never eat the same thing twice.

"Come on," Mooch said. "Come on, Mags. Make a wish on the unicorn."

"I want too many old things," I said. "Where would I even begin? . . ."

Now I didn't believe a broken-down old unicorn could make wishes come true . . . not for a minute. But what if it could?

I just wanted to be like everyone else, living in a house big enough so we wouldn't be tiptoeing around Mama sleeping on the living-room couch in the middle of the day. Our house would be big enough. Mama'd have her own room, a room with one of those curved-out windows she likes, and she could sit in that window all day long without one of us kids pulling on her.

And Mama wouldn't even need to sleep in the middle of the day, 'cause we'd have enough money she wouldn't have to work at night. She wouldn't have to work at all if she didn't want to. But even if she wanted to work, she could get a good job, like Aunt Lainie. Not that crummy job she has now, running the machine at the mill.

I wanted to look and act and be just like the other kids at school and not be embarrassed about who I am. I looked down at my pants, cuffed almost to my knees to hide they were too short, and twisted the unicorn's horn in my hand.

"I wish I had some decent clothes to wear," I said. "Some nice, decent clothes to wear, so Patty Jo and Alice would like me. There," I said, dumping the unicorn back on Hannie. "I did it. You happy now?"

"Ohhh!" Mooch cried. "Come inside, Mags. Hurry!"

Mooch grabbed me and Hannie and dragged us up the steps of the trailer. My lunch bag hung out of his back pocket, flat and empty now.

Hannie lugged the unicorn in behind her.

"Leave that dirty thing outside," I whispered to Hannie, but she tugged it on through the door with her anyway.

"Where's Mama?" I asked, balancing my books on a pile of papers on the kitchen table.

"Come on!" Mooch insisted, still pulling on us.

In the living room there was a big box sitting on the couch where Mama sleeps. The bathroom door was near shut, and I heard Mama humming to herself on the other side of it.

"Mama's putting on clothes," Mooch said. "Aunt Lainie sent a whole box of clothes in the mail.

All the way from Baltimore. Mama's been in it all afternoon."

Mama had been dividing the clothes up. There were two piles—on one side of the box a great big pile that spilled over onto the end table, and a little pile over on the other side.

Mama opened the bathroom door. She wore a pink sweater with penguins on it. It was too pretty for painting. "Hi, you two," Mama said. "You're home early."

"No, ma'am," I answered. "It's regular time, maybe even a little late."

Mama uncovered the clock on the end table, where it was hid under a pile of clothes.

"Oh, good lord, I better quit fooling around with these clothes and get ready for work. Your Aunt Lainie's new job is so fancy, she can't wear none of her old clothes anymore. Just look what she sent us." Mama started back toward the bathroom. "That pile on the far end there is yours, Mags. You see if that stuff don't fit you."

Mama pulled off that pink sweater, the one with the penguins on it, and tossed it on over to my side of the sofa. "This one's too small for me."

"It's mine?" I asked.

Mama nodded, smiling. She pulled out a new sweater and a pair of pants from her pile.

Hannie moseyed over to the sofa, to see Aunt Lainie's clothes. She was dragging the unicorn along behind her.

"Where'd that piece of trash come from?" Mama asked, staring at the unicorn. Her voice had been soft and happy when she'd tossed me that penguin sweater. Now I heard that tired sound she gets when she's paying bills or when Hannie and Mooch are getting on her nerves.

Hannie poked my ribs with her elbow.

"We found it down to Newell's field," I said.

"Well, you can march it straight back to Newell's field if you don't mind."

"Hannie keep it, Mama?" Hannie pleaded.

Mama glanced at Hannie. "No, baby," she said. Then she turned to me. "If you think I'm letting you keep that dirty thing in this house, Margaret Wade, you've got another thing coming. Honestly, you know better than to let her bring somebody's used-up toy home with her."

Hannie's fingers dug into my arm.

"Mama . . . if we cleaned it up, it wouldn't be so bad," I said.

"Don't tell me what's bad. You think I don't know what's bad? Whoever dumped that thing down Newell's field was glad to be rid of it. Now, quit fooling around and get it out of here."

"Please, Mama," I begged. "For Hannie."

Mama squinted up her eyes at me. "I said no, and I mean no, Margaret Wade. Get on, and don't even think about going near those clothes from Aunt Lainie until you've washed up good, you hear?" Mama disappeared into the bathroom.

I scowled at Hannie.

"You hear me, Margaret?"

I looked over at that penguin sweater, all balled up on the edge of the sofa. I just wanted to touch it.

Mama poked her head out of the bathroom. "Get on now, all three of you. Just make sure you're back before I leave for work."

"Yes, ma'am," I said.

3

Hannie cried as she bumped the unicorn down the trailer steps behind her. "H-Hannie k-keep unicorn, Mags?" she asked, sniffling.

I felt crosser than broken bones, thinking about those clothes waiting in there for me, wondering if I'd ever get to try them on, thanks to Hannie and that stupid unicorn.

"I told you not to bring it in the house, Hannie," I said. "I told you."

Hannie started crying harder, and Mooch kind of leaned up beside her, looking all serious. I swear if they didn't look like Tweedledum and Tweedledee from the play at the high school last year.

"Look," I said. "Mama's right. The unicorn got

left in Newell's field 'cause it's wore out and nobody wants it, Hannie, and that's the truth."

"No!" Hannie said, shoving her fists into her ears. "Hannie want unicorn."

Hannie can be as stubborn as tar.

I looked around, expecting Brody Lawson to pop out any second, but there was still no sign of him. I started wondering if the unicorn was one of his tricks after all. I took Hannie's hands from her ears. "Well, Hannie, if we're not taking it back to Newell's field, what are we going to do with it?"

"We got to hide it," Mooch said. "So nobody steals it."

I couldn't imagine anyone wanting to steal that sorry old toy, but it didn't surprise me that Mooch would think such a thing. Mooch knows all about stealing. He's snuck in every house along our road just to get food. He does it while Mama's sleeping and we're at school. I caught him with Twinkie wrappers a couple times. Mama never buys Twinkies.

He got caught by the neighbors just down the road from Brody Lawson's house last year. They didn't call the police or anything, but they spread the word all over town that Mooch was a thief. It got so

I couldn't go anywhere without hearing about Moochie.

Brody told me if his parents ever caught Moochie stealing from them, they'd make sure he went to jail. I didn't tell Mama what Brody said. She was angry enough. Mama taught Moochie a thing or two about what happens to children that steal, and he said he wasn't ever doing that again, but sometimes I worry.

"Hide unicorn?" Hannie said.

"Where we gonna hide it?" I asked.

"Under the bed," Hannie said.

That's where Hannie hides everything—I mean everything, from half-eaten bread to dirty underwear.

"We can't hide the unicorn under the bed, Hannie," I said. "Not after Mama told us to get rid of it. If she found it under there, she'd tan us good."

"I know a place," Mooch said.

I raised up my eyebrows.

"I do," Mooch insisted. "But you have to promise not to be mad if I tell you."

"I'm not promising anything," I said.

"It's that place back up to the road, that sort of tunnel under the highway," Mooch said.

"That old drainage ditch?" I asked. "Moochie, you're not allowed up there. You know that."

Moochie looked down at his feet.

"Moochie," I said. "Have you been going up there?"

"We got to hide the unicorn somewhere, Mags," Mooch said.

"Well, you can just forget about hiding it there," I said. "That's all the way back up to school."

Hannie's eyes lit up. "School? Hannie go roundy-round?"

The roundy-round is one of those wooden things on the playground that spins in place. You sit on it, holding on to a metal rail while somebody else spins you until you get real dizzy. That's Hannie's favorite place to play. She'd live on that thing if they'd let her. Her teacher, Mrs. Zobris, has to pry her off it at the end of recess. When it gets to spinning, you can hear Hannie's laughter all the way to town and back. Mama says I'm not supposed to let her on it on account of she might let go and fall off, but Hannie's as stubborn as boot leather and I never can get her away from it.

I knew the place Mooch meant. It was a stinking

drainage ditch with concrete sides all scribbled where kids had spelled their worst words out in spray paint. Mama'd told Mooch never to go near there. "Everybody knows that place," I said. "What kind of hiding place is that?"

"You don't know nothing, Mags," Moochie said.

"Anything," I said, correcting him. "And I sure do. I know there's snakes and broken glass there, and you've got no business being there in the first place."

"I can go any old place I want," Mooch said. "And you can't stop me."

"You just watch your sass," I warned. "I can stop you fast as a sink plug. Don't push me."

"Oh, don't wet your pants," Mooch said.

I wondered how come he was two years younger than Hannie and acted ten years older than me.

Hannie pushed up alongside him. "Moochie hide unicorn?" she asked.

"Follow me," Mooch said, heading back up the road toward school.

"Now, just hold on," I said. "Who's oldest here anyway? I don't think that old place is any good. It's not safe there."

Besides, if we went up that way, Hannie'd beg

to go over and play on the roundy-round, and I sure wasn't crossing her over that whole highway myself. It was bad enough getting across it with a crossing guard.

I hated that road, with its two lanes going in one direction and two lanes going in the other and that little strip of grass between them. I don't know just where my daddy died on that highway, but I do know I wasn't taking Hannie across it all alone.

"Forget it, Mooch. We're not hiding it there."

"Yes we are," Mooch said. "Where else we gonna put it? Mama knows all our other hiding places. But down the ditch there's this good hole for hiding things."

I scowled, wondering what all that boy had been doing at the ditch, but he wasn't about to give me a chance to ask.

"I got a wish on the unicorn, Mags. And you got a wish. You got all them pretty clothes. But Hannie didn't get a wish. We can't let nobody else get Hannie's wish."

Moochie had a point, sort of. Not that I really believed the stuffed unicorn had any power or anything, or that it could make our wishes come true, but

Hannie believed it could. And she ought to have a chance at a wish. I looked at her, her head cradled in the dirty neck of the unicorn.

"Well . . . maybe," I said. "If we just shove the unicorn into that hiding space of yours, Moochie, and hurry back home. We wouldn't be hanging around there or going across to the playground or anything. You hear that, Hannie? No roundy-round. But before we go anywhere with that unicorn, we've got to disguise it."

"Skies it?" Hannie asked.

"Yeah," I said.

Brody hung around down at that ditch sometimes. Even if this unicorn wasn't one of his tricks, I didn't want him seeing me carrying it around. We could put the unicorn in a big old plastic bag. Then if Brody saw us, he wouldn't know what we had. He might just think we were taking a little trash to the dump.

"We don't want anybody seeing your unicorn, Hannie, and stealing it. If we wrap it up, it'll just look like a heap of rags we're carting away. It'll be safe. That is, unless you already know what you want to wish for. Then you can just make your wish and we'll leave the unicorn down Newell's field like Mama said. We can leave it for the next person."

"No!" Hannie cried. "Hannie's unicorn."

Shoot. I could see she was gonna be extra stubborn about that mangy old thing.

"Hide unicorn, Mags?" she asked as we lumped the toy into an old plastic garbage bag Mama'd left crumpled under the trailer steps.

"Yeah," I said, starting off toward the ditch. "As long as you two promise not to go anywhere near the road. Swear it."

"Pinky swear," said Mooch, reaching up to hook his little finger around mine.

"Pinky swear," echoed Hannie.

4

Hannie was set on carrying the bag filled with that old stuffed unicorn all by herself, so it took forever getting up to the highway. I kept looking for Brody, but for once he really must have been off somewhere minding his own business. We walked straight up the road past Newell's field without seeing anyone.

The traffic rushed like a storm up on the highway.

We cut along the side of the road and followed the trail to the drainage ditch. The water down the bottom was green slime and stinking.

Hannie hung back, holding the bag with the unicorn so tight that blue veins popped out along each of her arms. But Mooch eased himself into the tunnel and let out a whoop.

He turned back around to Hannie and me, grinning at his own echo, his hands on his hips and the freckles on his nose squinched up so tight they laid on top of each other. "See," he said. "I told you this place is good."

It didn't look all that good to me, especially the way Mooch was balancing himself inside that tunnel, where the cement walls rose from that skinny ledge. Below the ledge was a dirt bank with the stinking water at the bottom.

"Careful, Mooch," I said, edging closer. I wrapped my arms around myself, hunching against the roar of traffic above. The sooner I was gone from here, the better. Looking down into the greasy water made me feel dizzier than spinning too long on the roundy-round.

Moochie reached inside a hole you couldn't even see from the path. He was clearing a place out for the unicorn. He stood up, shoving his fist in his back pocket.

Moochie called from inside the tunnel, "Give it here, Hannie." He stuck his dirty hand out, reaching for the bag full of unicorn.

But Hannie refused to hand it over.

"Hannie, it'll be all right," I said.

"No!" Hannie cried, pulling back. She turned toward home, then stopped. There was someone in the path. From where I was standing, all I could see was a pair of legs and some fancy new sneakers. There was only one kid at school who had a pair of shoes like that.

"Hey, Margaret Wade, what you doing in there?"

It was Brody Lawson. He slid down the path, closer to Hannie. I hated the way his eyes were spaced so close together on his head and that his thick black hair was all ridgety from front to back. It made me plain sick just looking at him.

I felt trapped there, between the highway and Brody. "I'm not doing anything," I said.

"That's my ditch," Brody said. "You're trespassing."

I swear I wonder why the earth doesn't just open right up beneath that boy and suck him down inside it.

"This is not your drainage ditch," I said. "Nobody owns a drainage ditch."

"If I say this place is mine, it's mine, Margaret Wade. You hear?" He came a step closer.

Mooch moved in the tunnel behind me. I saw his hand tighten around a rock. He was taking aim at Brody.

"You leave my sister alone," Mooch said. "Don't you come no closer or I'll knock your stupid brains out."

"You better watch how you talk to me, boy," Brody said. "I'm thinking I might just tell my mama about you stealing the Twinkies right out of our kitchen."

"I did not!" Mooch said.

I looked at Moochie.

"I can prove it," Brody said. "I can prove you did it. You might just be going to jail pretty soon."

Mooch looked at me. "I did not steal, Mags."

Hannie looked scared. She started whimpering.

The whole school was going to hear about this tomorrow. Patty Jo and Alice, too, about my crazy sister and my crazy brother down in the drainage ditch.

"We're going, Brody," I said, helping Mooch out of the tunnel. "Don't wet your pants."

Mooch took my hand. His chin stuck out and quivered a little, but he didn't cry.

We started away from the ditch toward where Brody was standing in the path. The wind from the highway blew hot across the back of my neck.

"Wait a minute," Brody said. "What you got there in that bag?"

Hannie's fists tightened around the unicorn.

"Nothing," I said.

"I'm not letting you past until you tell me."

"It's none of your fat-butt business," said Moochie, glaring at Brody.

"It is if you found it down in the ditch," Brody said. "Everything in that ditch belongs to me. Come on, what you got?"

"You stupid turkey head!" Mooch yelled. "You want to know what we got? . . . We got dead bodies in there. I been chopping up all the bad people I know. We were just coming for you."

"You better watch what you say, boy," Brody said. "You just keep your mouth shut."

"If you want my mouth shut, then you better let me and my sisters by," Moochie said.

Brody glared at Mooch with those narrow eyes

of his, but he stepped aside. Hannie, Mooch, and I, we pushed right past Brody up the trail. I wrinkled my nose as we came by like I was passing skunk.

Hannie and I took turns carrying the bag with the unicorn back home. Moochie ran ahead and slipped into the house to see if Mama was looking and gave us the all clear. We shoved the garbage bag under the steps of the trailer alongside some junk Mama was saving for Judgment Day.

I washed up good at the kitchen sink: my face, my hands, I even splashed water on my hair. I wanted to be full clean of the highway and the ditch and Brody Lawson before I came anywhere near those new clothes from Aunt Lainie.

I never even dried myself off. I was heading straight for that penguin sweater when Mooch caught me by my pants pocket and yanked.

"I'm hungry, Mags," he said.

"Not now, Moochie!"

"But my stomach's turning inside out," he said.

Mama poked her head out of the bathroom. She looked so pretty with her makeup and her new clothes and all.

"Lordy, Mags, are you ever wet. What'd you do,

girl, get caught in a rainstorm? Dry on off now, and start some dinner up, you hear?"

"Shoot!" I muttered under my breath. I swear that pile of clothes picked itself up and moved a little bit away from me.

What kind of wish did I get on that unicorn anyway? The clothes were there maybe, but it didn't look like I'd ever get a chance to try them on. Why did I always have to be taking care of everybody else? Why couldn't I just once take care of myself first?

I turned around and found Hannie staring out the window at the porch steps.

"Get away from that window," I whispered. "Mama's coming out and she'll figure what we're up to, sure as sugar. Come on now, Hannie. Can't you listen just for once?"

5

Hannie followed me into the kitchen. I boiled some noodles till they got soft, and drained out the water, dumped a can of mushroom soup and a can of tuna in the pot, and put the pot on the table for Hannie to stir.

"Now, don't touch anything but the handle, Hannie," I said, pushing the pot in front of her. "You stir it up good so it all gets mixed."

Hannie stirred while I got out bowls and forks.

Mama kissed the tops of our heads and waved us all good-bye and rushed out the door to work. I held my breath as she drummed down the steps, afraid she'd notice the bag with the unicorn, but she didn't.

Hannie dropped her fork and scraped her chair

back as soon as Mama shut the door. I knew right where she was heading.

"Hannie, sit down," I ordered.

"Hannie get unicorn," she said.

"Not yet," I said, holding on to her. "Sit back down, Hannie. You want Mama catching us with it? She's not even out of the yard yet. After dinner we'll bring it on in here and see if we can clean it up a little. Okay? But first we got to give Mama a chance to get to work."

Hannie grinned with her mouth all white from a swallow of milk. "Hannie wait."

I leaned back in my chair. The clothes still sat there on the sofa. I guess I'd just have to wait too.

After supper we brought the unicorn into the bathroom and dumped it out of the garbage bag. I didn't think a year of scrubbing would make a difference, but Hannie was bent on getting it so Mama would let her keep it.

I was afraid it might just fall apart if we got it wet or scrubbed too hard, so we used a washrag to wet a spot and then went over it with an old toothbrush. Hannie stooped and stood and stooped and stood, fussing all around the unicorn.

"It's pretty special, Hannie," I said, scrubbing away. "Not everybody has a unicorn in their bathroom."

"Hannie's unicorn," Hannie said, grinning.

"Boy, Mags, if I had my wish back again," Mooch said, running his thumb over the wet toothbrush and spraying me, "I'd wish—"

"Moochie!" Hannie cried, tugging him away from the unicorn.

"I'm not taking your old wish," Moochie said, shaking Hannie off.

"It's okay, Hannie," I said. "He already made his wish. He can't take yours away."

"If I could, I'd wish Brody Lawson would turn into a cockroach," Mooch said. "Then I'd stomp him good."

"And you'd leave the mess for me, I bet."

"Bad wish, Moochie," Hannie said.

"Yeah," I agreed. "And bad wishes don't count. Not on unicorns anyway, right, Hannie?"

Hannie nodded.

"If I had my wish again, I'd—" I stopped.

"What, Mags?" Mooch asked. "What would you wish? Would you wish bad things on Brody too?"

35

"No," I said. "I wouldn't waste a good wish on Brody. I don't know. I just want things to be different . . . better. You know." I used my finger and my thumb to flick some water at Hannie and then at Mooch. They both squealed and flicked water back. I didn't mind if they got me wet. I was already soaked from working on the unicorn. "Doesn't matter anyway. It's Hannie's wish."

"Hannie's wish," Hannie said.

"Three wishes on a unicorn," said Mooch. "It's always three wishes in the stories, isn't it, Mags?"

"I didn't think you were paying attention when I read you those stories, Mooch," I said.

"Sure I was paying attention, Mags. Hannie's the one who don't pay attention."

"Doesn't," I said. "And she does, too. She knew all about this unicorn, didn't you, Hannie?"

Hannie nodded, smiling.

"Anyway, just one wish left on this unicorn, and that wish belongs to Hannie," I said.

"Hannie," Mooch said, coming up beside her. "How about you wish for a whole truckful of Twinkies, and all the candy bars at Lessing's store, and—"

"Hush up, Mooch," I said. "It's Hannie's wish.

She doesn't care a fig about your stupid old Twink-ies."

"Hannie's wish," Hannie repeated, dripping wet from messing in the water.

"That's right, Hannie," I said. "Do you know what you want to wish for yet?"

"Hannie want unicorn."

"Well, we're working on that," I said.

"Hannie keep unicorn," she said.

"Holy," groaned Mooch. "Does that count as her wish, Mags?"

I shrugged. What if it did? It wouldn't be so bad. Something about having that unicorn around felt real good. I didn't really believe this wishing business any more than I believed in the man in the moon. Moochie's wish for something to eat was easy to explain. He always wanted something to eat, and I always had a leftover sandwich. And my wish for clothes . . . well, that wasn't much more difficult. Aunt Lainie's box would have come today whether we'd found this old unicorn or not. But I guess it was working *some* kind of magic, 'cause I hadn't ever heard Hannie talk this much or look half so happy, not in a long, long time.

It took a while, but when we were done, that unicorn almost looked like something out of a store.

"Oooh," said Mooch, standing back and admiring it in the crowded bathroom. "It looks good."

Hannie grinned. "Hannie make good wish."

"What you gonna wish for?" Mooch asked.

Hannie shrugged.

We shook the dust out of the plastic trash bag and stuck the unicorn back inside it before we slid it under the trailer steps. "We'll leave it there, at least until we can talk to Mama about keeping it," I explained to Hannie. "You know how grumpy she is when she comes home after working all night. We'll ask her when she's feeling good tomorrow, after we get back from school."

"Okay, Mags," Hannie said, wrapping her arms around me.

I got Hannie and Mooch cleaned up and ready for bed. I listened while they said their prayers. Hannie said a blessing for the unicorn.

"You better be careful what you dream tonight, Hannie," Mooch said. "You might wish for something in your sleep and use the magic up before you know it."

Hannie's face wrinkled up.

"Don't pay him no mind, Hannie," I said. "Mooch and I, we were both touching the unicorn when we made our wishes, weren't we Moochie?" I scowled at him. "You just make sure you don't make a wish while you're touching the unicorn, Hannie, unless you really want it. Now you two get in bed. I've got work to do."

"I'm hungry," said Mooch.

I could have sent him to bed without feeding him, but he wouldn't have settled down till midnight. Walking slowly past the pile of clothes on the sofa and into the kitchen, my eye lit on that penguin sweater.

Hannie and Mooch pushed me past it, coming up behind me like a stubby little train.

I fixed Mooch a bowl of oatmeal with a teaspoon of sugar in it. Mooch dipped his spoon in the sugar bowl twice more before I could stop him.

Hannie's head drooped sleepily at the table, watching Moochie eat. I walked her into bed and covered her up.

"I'll be in in a little while, Hannie," I said, kissing her. "You get some sleep now."

"Hannie love Mags," she said, yawning.

"Yeah," I said, patting her head. "Me too, Hannie."

Across the hall, stretched out on his belly, Moochie was hanging over the side of his bed.

I straightened him out and tucked him under the blankets.

"You finish your oatmeal?" I asked.

"Yup."

"You soak the bowl?"

"Didn't have to," he said. "It's all clean."

I could just imagine. Knowing Moochie, he probably had licked the bowl clean.

"You really think the unicorn made our wishes come true?" Mooch asked.

"Sure," I said, not believing it but liking the way it was feeling in the house tonight, with the clean white unicorn close by. "You got your wish for something to eat, right? And I got something to wear."

"But those clothes were there before you made the wish," Mooch said.

"So was the sandwich," I said. "Maybe all wishes are like that, Moochie. Maybe everything we always wished for is waiting somewhere, waiting for us to catch up and make it come true."

"Then I'm going to wish Brody Lawson drops dead."

I sucked a piece of food from between my teeth. "Well, someday he will," I said. "But you don't need to take any credit for it."

"You think Brody will call the police on me, Maggie?"

"If you keep stealing he will," I said.

"I don't steal anymore," Mooch said. "Brody's a liar. He can't prove anything."

"That's good," I said, staring hard at him. "You just keep it that way. You hear?"

"Night, Maggie," Mooch said.

"Night, Mooch." I pushed back his dark hair and kissed his forehead like Mama does.

Heading straight for those clothes, I nearly jumped out of my skin when I found Hannie out of bed again and staring out the window into the dark.

"Come on, Hannie," I said, leading her back to bed. "Your unicorn's just fine out there. Don't you worry. You just get some sleep and dream about what you want to wish for, okay?"

"Hannie bring unicorn to school?"

Before we'd cleaned it up, I'd have said no right

away. But it did look pretty good, and there was less chance of Mama finding it if we took it with us.

"We'll see," I said, but I couldn't help thinking Patty Jo and Alice would get a kick out of seeing a unicorn, especially a magic unicorn that made wishes come true. And wouldn't I just have the proof with that brand-new penguin sweater? I was already planning my whole outfit for tomorrow. Between new clothes and a stuffed unicorn, maybe tomorrow'd be just the kind of day I'd been wishing for.

6

I made it into the living room in front of the pile of clothes without any more interruptions. There were four shirts, two pairs of shorts, and two sweaters. I laid each piece out on the back of the sofa. One of the sweaters was itchy and plain. But that penguin sweater felt soft as kitten fur.

I wanted to get right into trying those clothes on in the worst way, but that'd mean turning the bedroom light back on and maybe waking Hannie up. I thought I'd just let her get sound asleep before I went looking through the closet for outfits and all.

I left the clothes to lie on the sofa while I went in to do the dinner dishes, the whole time thinking how one of those shirts could match up with a pair of pants

I already had and how another shirt would go nice with a skirt Mama got me last year at a yard sale.

Moochie *had* licked his oatmeal bowl clean. I could have put it back on the shelf, but Mama would have caught me sure as sweat on a hot day. I slid the bowl into the sink with the rest of the dishes and washed up. I always wash up. There aren't many things that make Mama crosser than a sink full of dirty dishes staring her in the face when she gets home from the mill. I took my time cleaning the kitchen up good before checking on Mooch and Hannie.

Mooch had the blankets tugged over his head. I tucked them down under his chin and touched his hair. He didn't even twitch.

Picking Moochie's pants up off the floor, I yanked my lunch bag out to use tomorrow. A wad of Twinkie wrappers flew into the air and landed on the floor.

Shoot! Moochie'd lied to me. He *had* been up Brody's house. What was I gonna do with that boy? I tried to wake Mooch and tell him a thing or two, but he was sleeping sounder than a rock.

I remembered how mean Brody'd looked, standing outside the drainage ditch like he owned the world and me and Hannie and Mooch were so much scum needing clearing away.

Brody was always bad-mouthing me, looking up close at all the things wrong, like my clothes not fitting right or my skinny old flat body, and he noticed all the things wrong with my family, too.

Well, I didn't need any more of that kind of attention. I needed some good attention. Not dragging my slow sister around behind me, not sticking up for my thieving brother. Not looking like everybody's hand-me-down. I needed something good, that Patty Jo and Alice would think, "Now there's a girl to have for a friend." I needed to feel as good at school as that old unicorn had me feeling right here at home.

I slipped into one of Aunt Lainie's shirts. It smelled a little bit like perfume. The shirt matched up good with my best jeans. Turning back and forth, I studied myself in the bathroom mirror. Pulling off the first shirt, I folded it up and tried on the next one. I matched all of Aunt Lainie's clothes with things I already had. Some of those outfits came out looking good, good as store bought. But that pink sweater with the penguins was best of all. It came down long enough to hide the stain in my white pants from where I got some blood when I became a woman and all.

I set that sweater and my white pants out to wear tomorrow and headed back into the living room, looking out the window to where the unicorn waited in silence.

"Listen," I whispered against the glass. "I don't want to take anything from Hannie, but if you've got more than three wishes in there, I wonder if you could manage to get Patty Jo and Alice to like me. You hear that, unicorn? I'm not asking you to change my whole life or anything. Just let Patty Jo and Alice like me."

That dumb essay was all I had for homework, but it waited, fit to thump down on me and lick me good. Everyone in class had to write about their family. What could I say about mine? That we lived in a trailer where there wasn't room enough to take more than two steps without walking into something or someone? Old Brody and Patty Jo and Alice would be writing about how their mamas sit home waiting for them in their fine, big houses and serve them Twinkies when they get back from school and cook them dinner, and tuck them into bed each night. And how they go on family vacations to places you can't even get to but on an airplane. And how their daddies have these big important jobs and make so much money they get a whole roomful of presents at Christmas. Shoot. I didn't even have a *daddy* at Christmas— not for a heap of Christmases, as a matter of fact.

I guess maybe I had my mind more on all of them at school than on my own family and my essay, 'cause I wasn't half done when Mooch's night terrors started.

He has them near every night. When he gets to hollering I go right to him, but as long as he's asleep he doesn't hear me.

I ran into his room and found him thrashing around in bed. "They're coming to get me! They're coming to get me!" He was screaming so loud, I guess Mama could nearly hear him up at the mill. Mama knew about Moochie's night terrors, but she said there wasn't anything we could do about it. She said Moochie'd grow out of it someday. I wondered if she was right. Mama said night terrors just happened to some kids, that Cousin Willy had had them and Aunt Lainie took him to all kinds of doctors there in Baltimore but no one ever could do a thing to stop them. He just grew out of it. I worried though that if Moochie was stealing again, his night terrors might be different from Cousin Willy's. They might be 'cause he was afraid someone really *was* coming to get him. Maybe he wouldn't grow out of them after all.

"They're coming!" Moochie screamed, swinging his arms up to protect himself. "They're coming to get me!"

"Who's coming, Mooch?" I asked, sitting on the edge of the bed, trying to untangle his blankets from around him and wake him up out of his nightmare. He was dripping with sweat.

"No!" he screamed even louder, fighting me off.

Hannie limped in, sleep droopy, and stood beside me. "Moochie scared?"

I nodded yes.

Hannie thumped over and tugged on Moochie's pajama sleeve. She yelled right in his ear, "Wake up, Moochie! Moochie all right. Mags here. See!"

Moochie looked at Hannie and blinked.

He started crying, awake crying, not nightmare crying. It was all right to hold him now. I cuddled him up and rocked him back and forth just like Mama does. He panted like an old dog.

"It's all right now, Moochie," I said.

"All right, Moochie," Hannie crooned.

Hannie slipped into bed beside Mooch, and I tucked them both up together and sat down on the edge of the bed, brooding on that half-finished essay, waiting until they were both asleep before I turned out the lights and got into bed myself.

7

Next morning I rolled that penguin sweater over my head and smoothed it down, turning this way and that in the bathroom mirror, trying to get a good look at myself coming and going. I flattened the sweater over my chest, looking for signs that I was growing some up top, but I hardly even showed. Patty Jo and Alice already wore bras, but I barely had enough to fill a teaspoon.

"Ohhh," said Hannie, barging into the bathroom without knocking. "Mags pretty."

I grinned. New clothes. Just like I'd wished. Maybe I did look good enough that Alice and Patty Jo would notice. I tiptoed past Mama sleeping on the sofa and got breakfast for Hannie and Mooch.

"You lied to me last night, Mooch," I whispered. "I found those Twinkie wrappers in your pants pocket. What are you going to do when some grown-up catches you stealing? 'Cause you know somebody's bound to. It's wrong to steal, Mooch. *Wrong!* Even if you're turned inside-out hungry and there's nothing in the house but cold spinach and ketchup, you got no right to take what doesn't belong to you."

"I *didn't* take anything! Brody Lawson's a liar."

"Then where'd those Twinkie wrappers come from?" I asked.

"I just got them, is all. Just let Brody try proving I stole them Twinkies. I'll stomp him to smithereens."

"How're you gonna do that?" I asked.

"I'll take Hannie's wish," said Mooch. "That's how."

Hannie started crying, but I shushed her before she could wake Mama.

"You can't have Hannie's wish," I said. "That's stealing too, and you can't do it. Not if I have anything to say about it."

"Well, I bet the unicorn would stomp on Brody even if I didn't wish it, 'cause unicorns are good and Brody's bad. Bad as dog breath."

"You just stay close to the house today, Mooch," I said. "Don't go near Brody's, you understand? Unicorn or no unicorn, you're going to end up in a hill of trouble if you don't quit stealing from people."

"I'm not stealing!"

"Okay, okay. We'll talk about it later, Mooch. Right now I got to get to school. Come on, Hannie," I said, smoothing her hair with my hands the way Mama does when she doesn't have time to brush it. "We've got to get moving."

I slipped my half-finished essay into my notebook, figuring how I'd work on it before school and during recess. Moochie blocked the way out the door.

"You taking the unicorn with you?" he asked.

Hannie looked up at me, her dark lashes touching the fringe of her bangs, her mouth sweet and round like a pink-iced doughnut. I know it's stupid, but when she looks at me that way, I feel like I could do anything.

"Yeah," I said. "As a matter of fact we are. We leave it here and you're sure to get in trouble with it."

"Take me to school too," he said.

"Moochie, we've been over this before. You're too young. Next year you go to school."

"I'm smarter than Hannie, and she goes to school."

"You just have to be six, is all," I said. "Doesn't matter how smart you are. You have to be six."

"I am six," Moochie said. "I've been six a long time."

"I know that," I said. "But you had to be six before school started last September, and you weren't six then."

"I don't want to stay here alone," Mooch said. He socked me on my behind, not so hard it hurt but so I knew he meant business.

"Well, you just have to," I said, watching Hannie drag the garbage bag out from under the porch steps. "We'll hurry home soon as we can."

I had to pull him off me, where he was clinging like an old bean creeper to a pole.

"I'm still hungry, Mags," he called after me.

"Hush now, Moochie," I said, warning. "Don't you wake Mama. Eat yourself some crackers. Mama'll be up in time to make you lunch, and I'll make you something special when I get home. Now stay out of trouble, understand?"

"Moochie sad?" said Hannie, dragging the plastic bag full of unicorn behind her.

She took hold of me with her free hand and swung my arm back and forth as we walked toward school.

"He's just lonely," I said. "It's hard, him being the youngest and having to wait home and no one to play with. Mama's just too tired from work to pay him any mind. And he's smart, too. Smarter than a lot of kids in my class even. Smart enough to get himself in some kind of trouble."

"Hannie not smart." Her face hung loose like she didn't have any bones under her skin. She had my sweater twisted in her sweaty fist.

I couldn't decide whether to say something nice to her or yell at her for stretching out my sweater, but before I could say anything at all, a rock rolled up alongside us. I stooped and picked it up and turned it round in my hand. A rubber band held an old Twinkie wrapper onto the rock.

I turned and looked back down the road behind me to where that rock had come from. Brody Lawson stood there, his hands on his hips, glaring.

8

"**S**hoot!"

I dropped that rock like it was a hot potato and refused to look back at Brody again.

Hannie was still dragging the trash bag along the ground.

"Get that bag off the ground, Hannie," I said. "Look what you're doing to it. You've got a hole worried in it so big, that unicorn's gonna fall out and get lost. Come on! Hurry up, will you? The crossing guard won't be there all day. I swear, you are the slowest . . ."

I tried ignoring that sad face of hers and pried her hand off my sweater for the umpty-dozenth time.

"Unicorn heavy, Mags," she whimpered.

"Then you shouldn't have asked to bring it in the first place . . . and you shouldn't have said you'd carry it by yourself."

I squinted toward the highway, trying to figure out who the crossing guard was this morning. I liked it when Mrs. Clinton crossed us. Hannie was scared of her, but she was just right in my book. She was bigger than a barn. Not even a stream of cars on the highway would mess with her.

"Use *two* hands to carry that bag, for crying out loud," I said, feeling angry at everyone in the world. "Can't you use your *head* sometimes, Hannie?"

I was so angry and I didn't even know why. I just knew it was all tied up with Hannie and Mooch and that scumball Brody Lawson.

The road roared in front of me with rush-hour traffic. It wasn't even Mrs. Clinton crossing today. It was crummy Mr. Bumbaugh, and him no bigger than Mama in her bare feet.

I hate that highway.

Mr. Bumbaugh got Hannie and me halfway across to the grass strip and then left us there to bring Brody over. I felt pulled apart, with the traffic tearing behind me in one direction and tugging the front of me in the other. We were later than ever this morning; nearly everyone was already out on the playground, waiting for school to start. I promised myself that when Mr. Bumbaugh held up traffic in the other direction, I would not run across in front of everyone. Running showed you were scared.

"Mags?" I felt Hannie pulling at the bottom of my sweater.

I turned around to look at her and found Brody Lawson's ugly face staring straight at me.

I pried Hannie's fingers off my sweater. It's bad enough she sticks to me like a sorry old shadow. I don't need her clinging on to me in the middle of that stinking highway in front of the whole school.

I scowled down at her and wished she'd just stay there, stuck in the middle of that road forever, and never bother me again. I felt my insides shivering and I wrapped my arms tight around my chest, so Brody wouldn't see I was scared.

Hannie was crying real soft, but I couldn't give in to her. Not with Brody standing there. She got louder, so that kids on the playground were starting to look up.

"All right!" I yelled.

Hannie jumped. I grabbed for her to keep her from stumbling back into the traffic behind her.

"Give that bag to me," I said. "I'll carry it."

I don't think she wanted to hand it over anymore, but she did what I told her for once. I could feel Brody behind me, burning holes in the back of my head with his narrow little eyes.

Some magic, I thought, holding the bag full of unicorn and feeling the ground shiver under my feet.

Mr. Bumbaugh held up his stop sign, stopping the traffic in the other direction. He waved us across.

I ran, even though I'd promised myself I wouldn't. I ran, with the bag full of unicorn bumping against my legs, until I felt the dirt and grass of the school yard under my feet.

I left Hannie off at her classroom. She reached for the bag with the unicorn, but I wouldn't give it to her. I wanted to show the unicorn to Alice and Patty Jo first, before I handed it over to Hannie and let her wreck it.

"I'll give it to you later," I said.

Hannie was still crying.

I felt worse than sour milk on an empty stomach, but Alice and Patty Jo were heading in from the playground toward the bathroom, just like they always did first thing in the morning, to put on their makeup and do their hair.

Today, in my penguin sweater, I felt good enough to be in there with them.

I ducked into the girls' lavatory and started fooling with my hair, when Alice and Patty Jo pushed their way in. They came in talking about a television show they'd seen last night, and I sort of pretended like I was listening and that I agreed with whatever it was they were saying. We didn't own a television, not since our old one died on us last year.

My heart was pounding as I waited for them to notice me.

I didn't wait long.

"Oh, Maggie," Patty Jo said, turning to take a closer look at me. She'd rinsed her short brown hair with something that made it look blond under the bathroom light. Mama would surely kill me if I ever colored my hair. But Patty Jo always did things like that. "I love your sweater. Where'd you get it? I want one just like it."

"You like it?" I asked, grinning at my skinny self in the bathroom mirror. I didn't want to say anything stupid, so I was afraid to say anything at all. Alice wasn't looking any too pleased about my being there.

"It—it's a real special sweater," I said, forcing myself to say something. "One of a kind."

I am so stupid! Why did I say something like

that? How did I know it was one of a kind? Just 'cause I never saw one before didn't mean there weren't hundreds just like it. I was sure Alice would catch me up in a lie.

Alice just rolled her eyes up in her head. She was shorter than Patty Jo and had long brown hair she'd curled on some sort of iron. Her face was round as a clock, with a nose stuck up in the middle of it hardly bigger than the end of my thumb. "What do you mean, one of a kind?" she asked. "Somebody make that sweater for you or something?"

I tried to keep my breathing even. At least Alice hadn't seen someone else wearing the sweater or seen it in a store somewhere.

"Sort of," I said. "It's got to do with what's in this bag here."

I pointed to the plastic trash bag. My hand was shaking, and I pulled it back close to my side before Patty Jo and Alice could notice. What if they laughed in my face when I told them about the unicorn?

"Oh, disgusting," said Alice. "You got the sweater out of a mangy old trash bag?"

"No!" I said. My voice didn't even sound like it belonged to me. It was high and shaky. "I didn't get the sweater out of the bag. What's in the bag got me the sweater."

"Shoot," Alice said. "I always knew you'd turn crazy in the head like your sister someday."

"Hannie is not crazy in the head," I said. "I'm not either. There's something magic in this bag. I can prove it."

"Sure," Alice said, turning away and ignoring me.

"I want to see, Maggie," Patty Jo said, her dark eyes curious. "What is it? What you got in the bag? Don't you even want to see, Alice?"

"All right," Alice said, turning back. "Let's see what you got in there."

My hands shook as I tried undoing the knot on the bag, and I ended up tearing a huge hole in it. I reached in and pulled the unicorn out, stuffing what was left of that sorry piece of plastic into the wastebasket.

"Ohhh," Patty Jo said. "Isn't it cute?"

"It's nothing but a stuffed animal for babies," said Alice.

"It's a unicorn," I said. "And it's magic."

Alice looked bored. "Sure," she said. "And I'm Tinkerbell."

"How do you know it's magic?" Patty Jo asked.

"I didn't have this sweater yesterday," I said. I explained about Hannie and the unicorn and making a wish.

"I just wished myself some new clothes, and there they were."

"Well, what else did you wish for?" Patty Jo asked.

I told her about Moochie wishing for something to eat.

"So what you gonna wish for next?" Alice asked.

"Don't know," I said. "Got any ideas?" I had a feeling that would get them.

"You mean you'd wish something for us?" Patty Jo asked.

"I might," I said, trying to ignore that choked-up feeling I get when I'm not being too honest.

"You're sooo lucky," Patty Jo said. "Everybody in school's gonna want that unicorn."

Alice put on her lipstick in the bathroom mirror. "That sweater is cute," she said.

I couldn't believe it. For Alice that was like saying "Let's be best friends." Thank you, unicorn, I thought.

Patty Jo reached out and stroked the unicorn like

it was something alive. "I believe it is magic," she said. "Even *you* look different this morning, Maggie. Doesn't Maggie look different this morning?" Patty Jo asked Alice.

I didn't give Alice a chance to answer. "I sure *feel* different," I said. Being with Alice and Patty Jo like that, I really did feel different.

"Can I try your sweater on sometime?" Patty Jo asked.

"Sure," I said. "You could even borrow it maybe. If I'm not wearing it."

"How you gonna keep someone from stealing that unicorn and making wishes on it themselves?" asked Alice, running her hand over the unicorn's horn.

I thought about Moochie wanting to turn Brody into a roach last night. "The thing about unicorn magic," I explained, "is it only works for good people wishing good things. Like if I wished something bad to happen to somebody, it just wouldn't happen and I'd probably lose my wish for good."

"How does the unicorn know if it's a good wish or a bad wish?" Alice asked.

"It's magic, Alice," Patty Jo said. "It just knows."

"Yeah," I said, relieved Patty Jo was on my side. "Just like that."

"So you're not wishing Brody Lawson would fall off a bridge and drown?" Alice asked.

Everybody knew I hated Brody worse than cold spinach.

"I may be wishing something like that," I said. "But I'm not wishing it on the unicorn."

Patty Jo laughed. Alice laughed too. They were laughing the way they do with each other, but with me standing right there.

"That's good you can't make bad wishes on it," said Patty Jo. "I can just think of some people I wouldn't want making wishes on it at all. Like my sister Loma."

"Yeah," Alice said. "Your sister Loma would wish you off the face of the earth."

The bell rang for school to start. I hadn't done any work on my essay, but I'd talked to Alice and Patty Jo, and I guess that felt more important than any old stupid homework. Patty Jo, Alice, and I walked to class together, all three of us in a row, with me in my pink penguin sweater in the middle, carrying the unicorn in my arms.

"You think you could come over to my house this

afternoon, Maggie?" Patty Jo asked. "You never been to my house before."

"Sure. I might," I answered, feeling fit to burst over being invited to Patty Jo's.

"My mama bought chocolate cake yesterday from the bakery," Patty Jo said, like maybe I needed some extra reason to say yes.

I thought about Moochie eating crackers. Maybe I could bring him home a piece of Patty Jo's cake wrapped in a napkin, if I handled things just right.

10

Mrs. Fribush smiled when we walked into the room. "Don't you look nice today, Margaret. What a pretty sweater. And is that your stuffed animal? I don't believe I've ever seen you bring anything from home before to share with the class."

I wanted to crawl under my desk. She made it sound like I was a baby, bringing my blanket to school for show-and-tell or something. Brody kicked the back of my chair with his foot.

Everybody was looking at me, but only Brody was being mean. Everyone else was smiling and fussing over the unicorn. I began to wonder if it really didn't have some sort of magic in it after all.

Mrs. Fribush finished taking attendance and

looked over in my direction. "Margaret," she said, "you may be class monitor while I walk the attendance down to the office."

Class monitor was usually Brody's job. . . . Not that he did anything—just that it was his job the same way that tunnel of concrete with the stinking water at the bottom was his ditch. "Class, I'll be collecting your essays when I get back. Use these few minutes to check over spelling, punctuation, and grammar."

Brody made a face at Mrs. Fribush's back as she walked out the door.

I got my essay out, trying to think of something to say in a hurry so I could finish it and hand it in.

Nobody else was even looking at their papers.

"That unicorn Maggie's got is magic," Patty Jo piped up. "That's how she got that new sweater and all. She made a wish on the unicorn and it came true."

"So that's what was in the trash bag," Brody said. He stood up and put his foot down on the unicorn's back, pushing, pushing till he'd flattened it to the floor.

"Hey, cut it out!" I said, scraping out of my chair and shoving him away.

The mark from the bottom of his sneaker stayed across the unicorn's back.

Brody came around the front of my desk. "If you got a magic unicorn," Brody said, "you better start wishing for more than clothes, Margaret Wade. You better wish for a short jail term for your brother. He's in a mess of trouble at my house, and he's gonna need a lot more than something to wear. Come to think of it, where he's going, they give them their clothes for free. Free black-and-white-striped clothes. You think that thieving brother of yours will look good in black and white?"

Everyone was listening.

I wanted to put my foot on his face and flatten him like he'd flattened the unicorn, but I was too embarrassed to move.

Alice pushed up against Brody. "Why don't you just shut up," she said. "You're always blowing off at Maggie about something."

"I'm not just blowing," Brody said. "Her brother *is* a thief. You remember he was stealing before? Well, now he's at it again. You should have heard my mama yesterday afternoon when she found a whole box of Twinkies missing. I bet he stole that unicorn from somewhere too."

"You don't know what you're talking about, Brody Lawson," I said.

"Heck I don't! Your brother's a dirty little thief. The lot of you are nothing but trash. My daddy said so. He said he ought to call someone and have that rusty tin trailer of yours towed away—with all you inside it."

I sat frozen in my seat. Kids started hissing all around me, saying how this was missing from their yard and that was missing from their room, and how maybe Moochie was behind all of it. Moochie would have needed a freight car to take everything he was accused of taking.

"He's been coming up to our house and stealing from us since he could walk," Brody said, getting everyone worked up, looking all around the room with those narrow eyes of his. "But yesterday he went too far, that's what my mama said, he went too far taking a whole brand-new box of Twinkies, and my daddy's going to—"

"What!" I cried. I felt like I was going to explode. "What's he going to do?"

"My daddy's going to see you pay for all the trouble you've caused," Brody said. "You're going to have to move away and never come back. And you'll never see your brother again, 'cause my daddy's going to see he gets locked up in prison for the rest of his life."

Alice snorted. "What world you living in, Brody? They don't put little kids in prison."

"Ever hear of the juvenile home, Alice? Huh?" Brody stuck his narrow little eyes up close to Alice. "That's worse than real prison. They chain those kids under porches. That's a fact. But that's nothing compared to what they're gonna do to Maggie's sister. She's going to a place for retards, and they'll never let her out. And her mama's going to jail for leaving her children alone all hours of the night and day. My mama says people go to jail a long time for that."

"Children," Mrs. Fribush said, coming through the classroom door. "What's going on in here?"

All the kids who had been staring at Brody swiveled back around in their seats, folded their hands, and looked straight ahead. "Nothing, Mizz Fribush." Mrs. Fribush glared at Brody as he slinked back to his seat.

But as soon as she looked away, Brody poked me with his ruler. "You just wait and see," he whispered.

I couldn't see anything but black, buzzing like bees in front of my eyes. I clamped my jaw shut to keep from crying.

"I'll be doing you a favor," hissed Brody. "You'll be rid of your stupid family once and for all."

"Margaret," Mrs. Fribush said. "Will you collect the essays, please?"

I scraped my chair back and grabbed my half-finished essay in my fist, but instead of collecting the other papers, I ran out of the classroom and flew down the hall to the girls' lavatory, where I knew even Brody wouldn't dare follow me.

I hated him. I hated him for saying those things. And I hated it most 'cause he was right. My brother was a thief. And my sister, she wasn't just slow. She'd never catch up, never. And my mama . . . where was she when we needed her? Other mamas were always around, why not mine?

I was sick and tired of trying to hold everything together, of cleaning and cooking and minding Hannie and Mooch. I pushed my fists into my eyes, trying to make the tears stay back.

Stupid, stupid essay. I ripped it into tiny little bits and dumped them into the wastebasket on top of the plastic bag I'd pulled the unicorn from less than an hour ago.

I hated that unicorn. We should have left it where it was, Hannie and I. We should have just walked past Newell's field and pretended like we'd never seen it. The unicorn did grant wishes, but not the way I wanted it to. It made people notice me all right, but they noticed all the terrible things about me. And it made me see myself too, really see myself and my family. No wonder people didn't want anything to do with us.

I swiped at my cheeks with the backs of my hands. I hoped somebody would take that lousy unicorn while I was in the bathroom, take it so I'd never have to see it again.

Mrs. Fribush must have been worried enough to send somebody after me. Patty Jo pushed open the bathroom door. She was carrying the unicorn.

"I thought you might like to have this," she said. "In case you wanted to make a wish or two about Brody or something."

I turned away from Patty Jo and the unicorn. I didn't want her to see me crying.

"It doesn't matter what Brody says." Patty Jo put an arm around my shoulder. She was trying her best to be nice.

"The police can't do what he said. You know that. They can't put a little boy in jail for the rest of his life for eating Twinkies. Honestly, Brody is so awful. He can't prove your brother's the thief. Maybe Brody's eating all them Twinkies himself."

I knew better. I'd found those wrappers in Moochie's pants pocket—not a whole box worth of wrappers, but enough to prove Moochie'd been into something he shouldn't have been into.

"You know what I think?" Patty Jo said, rubbing her hand up and down the unicorn's horn. "I think it's just that you look specially pretty today, Maggie, pretty as a peach, and that's what's got Brody all hot and bothered. My sister Loma says boys only tease you if they like you. That's why Brody's picking on you, Maggie."

I looked at Patty Jo in disbelief. And people thought Hannie was slow.

"Listen here," Patty Jo said. "You don't pay any attention to him. He's nothing but a stupid old bag of cooties. Come on back to class now. We just finished with our essays—"

"I ripped mine up," I said.

Patty Jo looked into the trash can, then back at me. "If you explain to Mrs. Fribush, she'll let you hand yours in tomorrow. I'm sure she will. Anyway, we need you to come back now. We're getting ready for group reading, and you read better than anyone else in class."

"You think so?" I asked.

"Sure. Everyone says you do."

Patty Jo handed me the unicorn.

I stopped outside Hannie's classroom door. Hannie's teacher, Mrs. Zobris, walked over when she saw me standing there.

"Could I give this unicorn to Hannie?" I asked. "It's really hers. She just let me borrow it for the morning."

Mrs. Zobris nodded.

Hannie grinned wide enough when she saw that unicorn coming. She latched on to it like a dog on a meaty leg. And there was that look in her eyes, that pink-icing look that always made me feel so good. Could what Brody said be true? Could they really take her away so I'd never see her again?

Back in my classroom I slid into my chair. Brody slouched down behind me with his long legs stuck out under his desk. I could feel him, kicking, kicking at my chair leg, but he didn't say another word.

11

At lunch recess I was glad to get out of the building and away from Brody. I leaned against the side of the school, listening to Alice go on about how her father said that if she didn't get rid of all her cats, he was going to drown them along with their kittens.

Patty Jo cried out, "Oh, Alice, how awful!" The sun caught in her short hair, making it look a little like a bundle of straw.

"Well, I don't know," said Alice. "They were real cute at first, but now we have cats all over the place and everything stinks like cat, inside and out, and the last litter, only one kitten came out normal. The other two were retards. Half the time they sucked on the mama's ears or tail instead of where they were supposed to suck."

I looked down at my feet. Patty Jo cleared her throat.

"Uh, um, Maggie," Alice said, squinting up at me. "I didn't mean anything about your sister. It's different with people, isn't it?"

I didn't want to get angry at Alice.

"I mean, it's not like I'm saying you should drown your sister or anything."

"It's all right," I said.

But what Alice had said made my stomach knot. Is that what people thought about Hannie? That she ought to be drowned? What was wrong with everyone that they would think Moochie should be chained in a hole just because he was hungry, or that Hannie should be drowned because she didn't understand some things as fast as other kids?

The sun burned through that penguin sweater, and my collar itched something awful. Sweat dripped down the back and the front of me, but I couldn't take the sweater off because the shirt underneath wasn't long enough to cover that stain in my pants. I shoved my sleeves up past my elbows.

"Hey, look." Patty Jo pointed to a bunch of kids pushing each other down by the roundy-round.

Patty Jo and Alice and I walked on over to see what the ruckus was about. Sounded like a cat fight, there was that much screeching.

"That's Hannie's voice!" I cried as we got closer.

Now I was pushing kids right and left, trying to get through the crowd. I expected to find Hannie all bashed up on the ground under the roundy-round, just like Mama said would happen. Instead I found her with her legs and arms wrapped tight around the rail. Wrapped right up with her was the unicorn. And Brody was standing over her, trying to pull it away.

"Give that here!" he was yelling. "You give that here, you retard."

Hannie lifted her face to the sky and howled.

"What'd you say!" I was madder than spit, pushing my way over to Brody.

"I said your sister's a retard," Brody said, staring me in the face. "A stupid should-have-been-dead retard."

I pushed Brody hard.

He stumbled backward and kids stepped away from us. I landed on top of him and slugged him good before he flipped me over and yanked my arm up behind me.

"Hey, leave her alone, Lawson," one of the boys said.

"Yeah," someone else called. "You're breaking her arm."

Someone pulled Brody off me. It hurt, I guess, what Brody had done to my arm, but I hardly felt it, I was that angry. Anyway, Brody backed off.

But the kids still stood all around with their mouths open far enough to catch flies. And then I noticed a trickle sound like water dripping, and people whispering and pointing, and Patty Jo and Alice were whispering and pointing too. They were pointing at Hannie.

Hannie sat on the roundy-round, and something was dripping underneath her. I swear I wanted to die. I wanted to shrink down into the dust and die.

Hannie'd wet her pants in front of the whole school.

Slowly she unwrapped herself from the roundy-round and limped over to me, clutching the unicorn under her arm.

"Hannie wet."

Kids were laughing at her now. It seemed like everyone was laughing at her. I stood up and brushed myself off. I didn't want to touch her.

"Hannie wet." She was crying now.

Part of me wanted to put my arms around her and comfort her. Part of me wanted to walk away like I never knew her, and keep walking. She smelled like pee.

I took Hannie by the hand and dragged her up to the girls' bathroom, where I cleaned her up good as I could. I rinsed out her panties and tried patting them dry with paper towels, but she still had to put them back on damp. She didn't like that any.

"Hannie go home?" she asked.

I shook my head no. The first time Hannie wet herself in class I took her home, but Mama sent us right back. She said Hannie only wet when she wanted attention, and if we let her come home each time, Hannie'd think wetting was a good way of getting what she wanted.

I brushed the unicorn off, but by now it didn't look much better than it did yesterday when we first found it. I'd have to scrub it down good again before we could show it to Mama.

"I'm not coming home from school with you today, Hannie," I said, steering her back to her room. "I'm invited with Patty Jo and Alice, and I'm going back to their house. You're going to have to get home all by yourself. You tell Mama and Moochie I'll be back in time to start dinner."

"Hannie go with Mags?"

"No!" I said. "You're not coming with me. You go straight home, you hear? I'll be back before dinner."

"Hannie wait here."

"No, Hannie," I said. "You can't wait. I don't want you waiting for me. You just walk home, straight past Newell's field, Hannie, and right on into the trailer. You know how to go. Moochie'll come after you before you're halfway there. Here." I pulled my lunch bag out. "You give him this. You do that, you hear, Hannie?"

"Hannie alone?" Her voice was small and scared, and she wasn't looking at me like she had earlier, when I brought the unicorn into her class. She was looking more like she had a bad pain somewhere.

"Look, Hannie. I'm giving you the unicorn," I said. "You're the one who figured out it was magic.

You hold on to it and nothing can hurt you. All you have to do is make a wish, and nothing bad can happen."

Hannie held the unicorn around the neck. "Okay, Mags," she said.

She was pulling at her damp undies when I left her off in front of her classroom, and I didn't see her again until school was letting out.

She'd forgot about going home alone. She came shuffling over to my class like she always did. I should have known she'd forget.

I was just coming out of the room with Alice and Patty Jo when I practically tripped over her.

"You're not thinking she can come, are you?" Alice asked, wrinkling up her bit of a nose.

"No," I said. "She's just going home now."

"If we hurry," Patty Jo said, "we can catch a ride with my sister over to the high school."

Hannie looked worried.

"Go on home, Hannie," I said, fed up with having to explain it all to her again just so I could go and spend a couple hours with my own friends. "Remember? You've got the unicorn. As long as you've got the unicorn, you'll be safe. All you need is to make your wish and nothing will hurt you. Go on, Hannie. Mama and Moochie'll be waiting for you. I'll watch till the crossing guard gets you over the highway. You got what I gave you for Moochie?"

Hannie nodded slowly.

Alice and Patty Jo were moving away, and I moved after them, turning to watch Hannie over my shoulder.

Hannie stared after me. "Mags!" she cried. "Mags, don't go!"

"You coming or not?" Alice called.

"I'm going, Hannie," I said.

Hannie latched on to the unicorn and started twisting it in her hands.

"Go on, Hannie!" I called.

I watched Hannie till she was safely across the road, and then I ran to catch up with Patty Jo and Alice.

12

I tried settling down in the backseat of Loma's car between Alice and Patty Jo, but I wasn't feeling all that good. I started thinking about how this maybe wasn't such a great idea after all. I wasn't even sure where Patty Jo lived or how I'd get back home from there. What if I had to cross the highway?

I'd never gone off like this. I didn't know what Mama'd say when I got home. I had the feeling she wasn't going to be too happy about me sending Hannie back by herself.

Patty Jo's sister hadn't been all that happy about giving us a ride. She wasn't even heading straight home. She had a friend with her and they were going to the friend's house so Loma could try out some clothes for a big party she had going on.

Loma drove along the highway with one hand on the steering wheel and the other playing with the radio. She hardly watched the road.

Loma's friend said something, and the two of them broke into snorts. Loma laughed so hard she headed into the other lane, and people honked at us till she straightened out.

Alice and Patty Jo leaned forward, listening to Loma's every word. It was hard to hear what they were saying up front, with the car being so noisy. It kept backfiring and sounding like the motor was somewhere under our feet.

Patty Jo's sister wore perfume so strong it made my head ache. It wasn't like the smell in Aunt Lainie's clothes. That was nice. This smelled like Loma'd taken a bath in room freshener. I asked maybe if she would open her window and let in some air. She looked over her shoulder at me like I was lamer than a three-toed frog, never watching the road the whole time. She said the wind would mess her hair up. Said, who was I anyway, and her friend stared at me a good minute before she turned around and started singing with a song on the radio.

Patty Jo and Alice and me stayed squeezed in back like pickles in a jar while Loma stopped the car and went inside her friend's house.

"Don't forget we're out here," Patty Jo called after her.

"You telling me what to do?" Loma called back. "If you don't like Loma's taxi service you can get out and walk."

"Don't you all have chores to do after school?" I asked after Loma and her friend disappeared into the house.

Alice snorted. "My mama won't let me do anything around the house. She says I can't do it right, so I might just as well not even bother."

"I got to clean my room sometimes," Patty Jo said. "But if I make up enough excuses and put it off long enough, my mama pays me for doing it, she's that glad to get it clean."

I liked being in that backseat with Alice and Patty Jo, listening to them talk. Even if we were crammed in. I felt like I really had myself a couple of friends. But I still kept worrying about Hannie, and how mad Mama was gonna be when I got home.

"Sometimes Loma pays me for cleaning her room," Patty Jo said.

86

"Do you do it?" Alice asked.

"Sure I do," Patty Jo said. "We're getting this ride aren't we? You don't think Loma'd give me a ride for nothing."

I did things for Moochie and Hannie all the time for nothing. I liked doing things for them.

Patty Jo pushed and pulled herself out of the backseat and slipped into the spot where Loma's friend had been sitting. She started nosing through Loma's glove box.

"Let's see what old Loma's got stashed in here," she said. She found some Band-Aids, a napkin for when you have your period, a wad of tissue, two Roy Orbison tapes, and something red and lacy.

"Ewww!" she squealed. "Look what I found! This is my mama's. I bet she's been looking all over for this. Wait till she finds out Loma took it."

Patty Jo held up a skimpy red bra she'd dug out from under all the junk in Loma's glove box.

Alice lunged forward and snatched the bra away from Patty Jo. They both squealed and carried on like they'd found a stash of money or something.

Clutching the bra in her hand, Alice pushed her way out of the car, protecting herself against Patty Jo's fists.

"Give that back!" Patty Jo demanded. "You give that back right now."

Alice stretched the bra across her chest and stuck herself out in front, strutting up and down the walk outside Loma's friend's house.

"Come on," Patty Jo said. "Let me have it. I saw it first!"

Alice blocked Patty Jo with her body every time Patty Jo made a grab for the bra.

"Alice!" Patty Jo said. "It's not fair. Give me a turn!"

"Wanna try it on, Maggie?" Alice asked as she strutted past the car.

I turned near as red as that stupid bra.

Alice spun the bra over her head. I swear Patty Jo went for it just like a dog doing tricks, and each time Patty Jo tried grabbing it, Alice'd pull it away.

"It's my mama's," Patty Jo cried. "Give it here."

"It must be your mama's, cause it certainly ain't yours," taunted Alice. "You don't have anything to put in it."

"Do so!" Patty Jo cried.

"Where?" Alice asked, squinting at the front of Patty Jo's shirt.

They were arguing good when Loma came out. She saw Alice twirling the bra around on her finger and snatched it away and started yelling at Patty Jo and slapping her around for letting anybody touch it.

Patty Jo grabbed a handful of Loma's hair and yanked, and Loma scratched Patty Jo with her nails.

I got myself out of the backseat of that car and tried to stop them, but they kept coming at each other and I couldn't hold them back. Reminded me of two cats, the way they were carrying on.

I felt as tangled as a fly in a spiderweb, just watching them. Even when Hannie wet her pants and embarrassed me in front of the whole school, I didn't treat her like Loma was treating Patty Jo. At least, I hoped I hadn't treated her that bad.

"Just for that, you can walk home, Miss Patty Jo Widebottom," Loma said. "You and your stupid little friends can just walk home."

"You can't make us," Patty Jo said. "You've got to take us home."

"Like hell I do," said Loma. She slammed the car door shut and peeled away from the curb.

Alice shoved Patty Jo down in the grass. "Just great, stupid," she said. "Do you know how far we have to walk?"

"It's not my fault," Patty Jo said, crying. "You started it. You wouldn't give me that bra."

"I would have given it to you," Alice said, "if you hadn't acted like such a baby. You always act like such a stupid baby."

Patty Jo glared at Alice. "If you think I'm such a baby, why do you hang around with me, huh?"

"I don't know," Alice said. "I'm asking myself the same thing."

They'd forgotten all about me. I just stood a little away from the road, watching. I'd always thought Alice and Patty Jo were better than me. I'd wanted to be just like them. But now I was looking at them, I could see maybe neither of them was anything like I thought.

"I'd better be heading back home," I said. "I have to write that essay for Mrs. Fribush by tomorrow."

They didn't try to stop me. They acted like they didn't even know me in the first place, like, what was I even doing there?

It seemed to take forever getting back home. At least Loma's friend lived on the same side of the highway as me, so I didn't have to cross, but she lived far enough. There wasn't any easy way getting back.

I never was so glad as when I finally caught sight of Newell's woods. I started running through the trees, getting brambles stuck on my sweater. A loop of yarn snagged on a branch and got pulled, so it looked like one of the penguins was grinning. I was glad he was happy, 'cause I sure wasn't feeling any too pleased with myself.

The sun disappeared behind a big stretch of gray clouds, and I shivered. My shirt under the pink penguin sweater was soaked with sweat.

I remembered Hannie's damp undies and I couldn't help worrying about her. I felt the knot in my stomach tighten as I came in sight of the trailer. Something was wrong. I didn't know what. But just looking at it, I could tell. Something was wrong.

13

"Hey!" I called.

There was no answer.

"Hey, Hannie! Mooch!"

I thought maybe they were angry on account of I hadn't come straight home with Hannie. Mama was sure to be ripping. She'd probably be trying to get dinner at the same time she was getting ready to leave for work. Maybe Hannie and Mooch were so busy helping her in the kitchen, they didn't notice I was home.

But when I got inside the trailer, no one was there.

I came into the kitchen. On the floor was a balled-up scrap of paper. I picked it up and flattened it out on the table. It was a note written in Mama's scrawl.

> *Maggie,*
> *Mooch done bad. We're at the police.*
> *Take care of Hannie till I get back.*

Mooch . . . at the police. It couldn't be. He was six years old. Could they really put a six-year-old in jail, like Brody said? Could they do everything to my family that Brody said they'd do?

Mooch wasn't bad. He didn't belong in jail just because he was hungry. Couldn't people see that? That we were trying the best we could, me and Mama and Mooch and Hannie . . . .

Hannie! My heart started banging against my ribs like a fist at a door. Hannie!

Where was Hannie?

Mama had gone to the police with Moochie before Hannie'd come home. Why else would Mama have said "Take care of Hannie"? Hannie'd made it home all right. She'd made it home all by herself. But when she got here, there was nothing but an empty house. Mama and Moochie were already gone. Hannie'd found a note she couldn't read and no

Mama. That's why the paper was balled up on the floor.

I tore through the house, checking everywhere for her. Even under the bed. She wasn't there.

"Hannie!" I called.

I flew out the door and down the trailer steps. Maybe she was hiding under there, the way we'd hid the unicorn, but there was nothing.

I looked up and down the road and across the grass toward the woods, but I didn't see any sign of her.

Racing to the nearest house, I pounded on the door. Maybe they'd seen her. Maybe they'd taken her in. Nobody answered.

"Hannie!" I yelled.

I had told her she'd be safe as long as she had the unicorn. All she needed to do was wish on that unicorn and she'd be fine.

How could I have lied to her like that? How could I have taken a chance with Hannie?

I'd said those things to get rid of her. I'd done it so I could go with Patty Jo and Alice. And now Hannie was walking around out here somewhere with the unicorn, thinking she was safe, thinking she could do anything and she'd be fine, that all she needed was to make a wish and nothing could hurt her.

"Hannie!" I cried.

My voice bounced around the clearing.

Where would she go? I was pacing back and forth in front of the trailer now, trying to think where Hannie might be.

She'd be scared when she got home, and lonely. She'd go looking for someone. For me. And the last place she'd seen me was back to school. She'd have gone there, toward the highway.

It was late, so late the highway'd be roaring with cars. She couldn't possibly make it across on her own. I couldn't lose Hannie like this. We couldn't lose Hannie the way we'd lost my daddy.

Oh please let her be anyplace but near that highway.

I started running. A pain like the lid of a tin can sliced into my side, but I kept going. My chest burned like snakes of live wires. I still kept running.

"Hannie!" I called as I came down to Newell's field.

And then I saw it. The unicorn. It was propped up against the fence, looking just like it had when we first found it. Filthy and broken and unwanted. I ran over to it. I didn't care if Brody saw me. I didn't care if the whole world saw me. I took the unicorn up in my arms and held it to my chest, trying to feel Hannie in it, to smell Hannie, to touch Hannie.

"Hannie!" I cried.

But there was no answer.

"Please," I prayed, clutching the unicorn, gripping its horn in my fist. "Please let Hannie be all right. I wish it. I wish it with all my heart. If there ever was any magic, let there be enough left for this. Please let Hannie be all right."

I put the unicorn back against the fence post and turned toward the road. The traffic whined up on the highway. It was nightmare sound. It was the monster that came after me in my sleep, the way Moochie's night terrors came after him.

I could smell the stinking fumes and hear the bellyache of tires on blacktop. What I couldn't hear was Hannie. Not anywhere. There was no sign of Hannie.

14

I tried to block out the road sounds. I was listening for Hannie the way I listened for Moochie when I went to bed before his night terrors started. My ears strained, strained to hear all the bad sounds, all the danger sounds. My ears were listening for Hannie's danger.

I veered off to the side and went down the path to the drainage ditch, thinking maybe, just maybe Hannie was hiding down there.

"Hannie?" I called.

The ditch was empty. There was no sign of her. I was wasting time. Hannie would never come here. She was afraid of the ditch. She was afraid of Brody, too.

I tore back to the road, imagining Hannie hit and lying on the shoulder, broken, just like my daddy. Just like my daddy when he went out on the highway.

I was running, my eyes searching the road for a sign of Hannie. I didn't see the rock sticking up on the path until I'd tripped over it and twisted my ankle. A car came out of nowhere and whistled past me.

I pulled myself back up. The foot I'd twisted wouldn't hold my weight. Tears boiled up behind my eyes and I didn't even try to stop them from falling. I didn't care if the whole county saw me crying. It didn't matter what anyone thought about me anymore.

I just kept searching the highway for Hannie. And then something across the road caught my eye. Someone was on the playground, someone small and alone, sitting on the roundy-round.

"Hannie!" I cried. "Hannie!"

I was so relieved to see her. Hannie was all right.

But there was a whole highway between us. Cars, endless lines of cars, spun out down the highway. It was late afternoon and the sun hung low in the sky, making the drivers squint their eyes down to slits. Hannie rose up from the roundy-round like some awkward bird and ran toward me, her chunky legs and arms flapping as she went, her short dark hair flying every which way. She ran straight toward the traffic.

"Hannie! Hannie!" I screamed, trying to make her see the danger. But it was too late. Hannie ran out into the road.

Tires squealed and horns blared. A car swerved around her.

But a moment later the traffic started moving again, moving back and forth around Hannie as she stood trembling on the strip of grass dividing the highway.

"Hannie, stay there!" I screamed, pushing the palms of my hands at the air as if I could hold her back from the danger. "Stay right there!"

I didn't have to tell her. My sister stood, her arms flapping, her dark hair wild with the wind, her legs dancing with panic. My sister stood with her face turned toward me, looking at me like I could do anything.

Like I could do anything. Well, I can do most things, but one thing I cannot do is cross this highway. I'd do anything for Hannie, anything. But I cannot cross this highway.

"Mags!" Hannie was pleading.

Cars were honking at her and she stood in the same spot but always moving, like in a nightmare when you're scared but no matter how hard you try to run away your legs won't go.

"Hannie!" I cried back. "Stay where you are."

I tried again to put weight down on that twisted ankle, but the pain screamed up my leg and made my fists tighten.

"Mags!" Hannie cried. "Mags take Hannie!"

"I can't, Hannie," I called back. "I can't—my ankle."

But it wasn't my ankle keeping me from getting to her. It was the road. I was afraid of the road.

"Mags!" Hannie's cry ripped across the roar of the traffic.

I had to go out there and get her. I had to break into that string of cars and trucks tearing past me and get Hannie out of the middle of the road, where I'd wished she'd be stuck forever a million years ago this morning.

I was breathing like a freight train, short, tight breaths, and they weren't getting me air enough to fill a straw.

I saw a break coming in the traffic and I put one foot on the road. But the next car, it was coming so fast and my ankle burned so bad. I couldn't get out there.

Hannie was howling, howling worse than Mooch in his worst night terrors.

Another break in the flow of cars. I could do it. I could get her.

"I'm coming, Hannie," I called. "Wait there. I can get you."

And I tried. I did. I tried. But I kept seeing the unicorn flattened under Brody's shoe. I kept seeing Mooch in prison. I kept seeing my daddy's back as he headed toward the highway.

"Hannie!" I cried.

She stopped howling. She looked at me . . . she looked at me and really saw me. The look in her eyes wasn't a look that said I could do anything. It was a look that said she needed me.

"Maaagsss!" she wailed.

"I'm coming, Hannie. I'm coming."

I didn't wait for a break this time. I rolled that sweater up over my head and started waving it. I waved it at the oncoming traffic the way Mrs. Clinton, the crossing guard, waved her stop sign. I waved my sweater and limped up onto that highway.

Cars screeched. The sound of a semi's air horn

split through the hazy afternoon. A car skidded onto the shoulder, spitting gravel, but it finally stopped. The traffic ground to a halt, and slowly, slowly I made my way across, one step at a time, waving that penguin sweater while the traffic waited. My eyes were fixed on Hannie, waiting for me out on that little grass strip in the middle of the highway. I reached out and took her hand and pulled her to me. And still holding up my sweater with one hand, I led Hannie, step by step, with that wall of cars and trucks hanging over us. Step by step we made our way out of the middle of the road and back across, where we belonged.

"Hannie," I said, letting out my breath for the first time since I'd started out to get her. I held her safe against me and felt her heart pounding. Her chunky little body gave a shiver, and I wrapped my arms tight around her and rocked her back and forth, back and forth. "It's all right, Hannie," I said, my tears dropping in the dust on the path beside the highway. "It's all right."

And it really was. "Come on now, Hannie," I said. "It's time to go home."

15

As we went past Newell's field, Hannie and I looked over to the fence post at the same time.

"Gone," Hannie said. "Unicorn gone. Good-bye, unicorn."

I looked over to where I'd seen that unicorn, where I'd held it and wished for Hannie to be all right. Even in the fading light, I could see it was gone.

"Hannie make wish," Hannie said. "Hannie make wish on unicorn."

"Is that why you left it here, Hannie?" I asked. "You made your wish and then you were finished with it?"

Hannie nodded.

"What did you wish for, Hannie?"

"Hannie wish Mags back."

I put my hands on her shoulders.

"You used your wish for that, Hannie?" I asked. "You wished for me?"

Hannie nodded. "Hannie wish for Mama and Moochie and Mags."

She hadn't just wished for me. She'd wished for all of us. Hannie understood better than I did that we were all important. We were family.

We walked up to the fence post where the unicorn had been only an hour ago.

"Good-bye unicorn," Hannie said.

"Yeah," I said, touching her dark hair. She'd been saving her wish. She'd been saving it so she could keep that unicorn. But she'd found something she wanted even more. I had too.

We were nearly to the trailer when Mooch banged out the door and raced to meet us.

"Mooch," I cried. "You're home!"

Hannie hugged Mooch and danced him around in a crooked little circle.

"Course I'm home," he said. "Where'd you think I was?"

"What're you talking about, Mooch?" I asked. "I thought they put you in jail for stealing."

"I never took those Twinkies," Mooch said. "Brody just said I did. He said I took other things too, but I didn't. He made his mama call the police on me."

"Then how'd you get those wrappers in your back pocket, Moochie?" I asked.

"I just found the wrappers down in the ditch under the highway, Mags. Sometimes there's a little bit of cake left on the wrapper and I lick it off. That's not stealing."

"Then you weren't lying?" I asked.

"Heck no," Mooch said. "You and Mama told me no more stealing, and I didn't steal no more. I just didn't want Mama thinking I was eating somebody's old trash."

"Well, how'd those Twinkie wrappers get down to the drainage ditch in the first place?" I asked.

"Brody took them, Mags," Mooch said. "He took beer and stuff there too. I saw him. And he knew I saw him. He said if I told anyone, he'd make it look like *I* took all that stuff."

"Why didn't you tell on Brody before?" I asked.

"Well, I knew I'd catch it if you found out I'd been down to the ditch."

"You're right about that," I said. "You should have never been down there in the first place, Mooch. Mama and I, we told you not to go down there. And I don't want you going back there again either, you hear? That place is good for rats and snakes and nothing more."

"Ditch good for Brody," Hannie said.

I grinned. "You made a joke, Hannie! That's a good joke! You're right. That drainage ditch is good for three things: rats, snakes, and Brody Lawson."

I put one arm around Mooch and one around Hannie, and we walked back toward the trailer, three in a row, with me in the middle—limping on that bad ankle—dragging my filthy pink penguin sweater behind.

"Was Mama mad about going to the police station?" I asked.

"Ohhh," Mooch said. "She was boiling. Mama told the Lawsons a thing or two when she found out what Brody'd been up to. It wasn't nice what Brody's daddy did to Brody either."

"I just bet it wasn't," I said.

"We got to ride home in a police car, Mags. The policeman let Mama and me sit in front with him. I made the siren go off by the Lawsons' house and Mama started getting mad, but the policeman laughed and Mama wasn't as mad as I thought, 'cause then she started laughing too."

We climbed the steps to the trailer and went into the kitchen. Mama was at the stove, cooking dinner.

"I can do that, Mama," I said. "You're awful late for work."

"I already called," Mama said. "I'm not going in tonight."

She smiled like she didn't even care about a short check this week, and I smiled too for having Mama home, cooking dinner and taking care of us.

I went up and hugged Mama right then and there with her back to me standing at the stove, and Hannie came up and hugged her too. And then Moochie joined in, and Mama laughed like slow music and said, "You kids," and kept on cooking.

Later that night, while Mama sat outside on the porch steps, Hannie, Mooch, and I, we piled into bed. We were all feeling good, with our bellies full and Mama right out front waiting to tuck us in and kiss us good night. Mooch asked a million questions about the unicorn. Hannie's eyes lit up, and she started chattering like a squirrel in a gum tree.

Mooch wriggled around, digging his old elbow into my side. "Hey, Mags," he said. "You think maybe Mama being here, and Hannie so happy and all—you think maybe that's a little magic the unicorn left behind?"

Hannie'd been messing around under the blankets. She came up grinning, her hair poking every which way.

"Could be, Moochie."

Mama pushed the screen door open and called in for us to settle down and get ourselves to bed.

"It could just be," I said.

GO FISH

KAREN HESSE

What did you want to be when you grew up?
Braver.

When did you realize you wanted to be a writer?
I can't remember a time when I didn't want to write.

What's your first childhood memory?
Going to the hospital to have my tonsils removed. I was three.

What's your most embarrassing childhood memory?
There are so many. One of the most memorable was the time I gave a classmate a black eye.

What's your favorite childhood memory?
One of my favorites is going out to eat at the Pimlico House with my mother, my grandmother, and my aunts. I was the only child and I wore white gloves and white anklets and shiny black patent-leather shoes. I felt so grown-up.

As a young person, who did you look up to most?
Everyone. But particularly my grandfather. He was so kind.

What was your worst subject in school?
MATH!!!

What was your best subject in school?
Everything else. I LOVED school.

What was your first job?
Bagel Shop waitress.

How did you celebrate publishing your first book?
We splurged and my husband, my two daughters, and I ate in a restaurant . . . a very rare treat.

Where do you write your books?
In the attic of my 1880, Queen Anne house.

Where do you find inspiration for your writing?
Everywhere. Newspaper and magazine articles, radio and television interviews, lectures, art, music, overheard conversations, other writers' books, life.

Which of your characters is most like you?
Emily Michtom.

When you finish a book, who reads it first?
That all depends on who's running the slowest.

Are you a morning person or a night owl?
Definitely morning.

What's your idea of the best meal ever?
A dark chocolate appetizer followed by a dark chocolate entrée, finishing with a dark chocolate dessert washed down by a rich pot of chocolate and a few hours later, a couple of aspirin for the sugar headache and digestive aids for the obvious reasons.

Which do you like better: cats or dogs?
I adore them both!

What do you value most in your friends?
Honesty and a sense of humor.

Where do you go for peace and quiet?
Inside myself.

What makes you laugh out loud?
My husband.

What's your favorite song?
Too many great ones. But I have a major soft spot for anything by James Taylor.

Who is your favorite fictional character?
Too many great ones. But I have a Very Soft Spot for Horton (of Hatching the Egg fame).

What are you most afraid of?
I'm too scared to tell.

What time of year do you like best?
Spring.

What's your favorite TV show?
I'm pretty enthusiastic about *The Charlie Rose Show* on PBS. But I've also been caught watching Oprah from time to time.

If you were stranded on a desert island, who would you want for company?
My husband.

If you could travel in time, where would you go?
I would go to the beginning of the universe with Dr. Who.

What's the best advice you have ever received about writing?
Don't quit your day job.

What do you want readers to remember about your books?
I'd be delighted if readers remember anything about my books.

What would you do if you ever stopped writing?
I can't imagine not writing.

What do you like best about yourself?
My crazy, curly hair. Ironically, it's the thing I liked least about myself when I was growing up.

What is your worst habit?
My husband says I have none. Ha-ha.

What is your best habit?
My husband wouldn't say, but I suspect I have none of those, either.

Where in the world do you feel most at home?
Brattleboro.

What do you wish you could do better?
See through walls, fly, and cook.

What would your readers be most surprised to learn about you?
That I have a sense of humor.

The guys say I'm lucky. That I got everything.

They're right. I am lucky.

I'm the luckiest kid in the world.

Not everyone's so lucky. I know this.

Take Dilly Lepkoff. Dilly pushes his cart past our store every day, rain or shine. Dilly, in his long apron, he calls, "Pickles! Pickles!" Just hearing his voice I'm drooling, tasting the garlic and vinegar across my tongue. Those pickles of Dilly's, they suck the inside of your cheeks together. They make the spit go crazy in your mouth.

So Dilly, he knows what he's doing with a pickle. But is he lucky? That all depends on what you call luck. He and his family, they been to Coney Island, which I have not. That makes him lucky in my book. But Dilly Lepkoff, he's still looking for a land of gold.

In the Michtom house we got golden land coming out our ears. Does that make me lucky? Ever since school let out I been asking Papa to go to Coney Island. And always the same answer. "We're too busy, Joseph. Maybe next month."

On the corner of Tompkins and Hancock, Mr. Kromer's clarinet cracks its crazy jokes. Mr. Kromer plays that clarinet all day. He stands under the grocer's awning in his gray checked vest and he plays good. Makes you smile. Makes your feet smile. I hear it, even when I'm playing stickball with the guys halfway down Hancock. Even when I'm planning how to sneak into Washington Park to watch the Superbas. I hear it. Mr. Kromer really knows how to stir up something with that clarinet.

But does that make him lucky? In Russia he played clarinet for important people. Now he plays on a street corner in Brooklyn and he keeps the clarinet case open for people to drop coins. I'm not sure, but if you asked Mr. Kromer I don't think he'd say he's so lucky.

Papa, he's lucky. He doesn't work for coins anymore. We're not greenies. Not anymore. Papa, he's been in America sixteen years.

"And I didn't have a penny when I got here."

"You had to have something, Papa. How could you live if you're dead broke?"

"I lived, Joseph. I'm here, am I not?" Papa says. "And I had nothing." Only he says "nuh-tink."

You get used to it. Everybody got an accent in Brooklyn. Everybody talks a little different. Papa says he doesn't hear a difference but I do. Same as I hear Mr. Kromer's clarinet. You gotta listen.

I can't remember living anywhere but Brooklyn. Only here, above the store, in this crowded flat. Me, Mama, Papa. My kid sister, Emily. My little brother, Benjamin. I like coming home to this place. At least I used to like it. Back when we sold things like toys and cigars and paper, back before we turned the candy shop into a bear factory. Our novelty store with the big glass window, it's always been like an open book. The whole block, like a row of glass books on a long cement shelf. Even though lately we don't fix up the display window, I guess I still like coming home to it.

Some kids, they never want to go home. This time last year I didn't get it. How could anyone not want to go home? I get it now.

Still, I'm lucky. My life, it's better than most guys have it. I got plenty to eat. I got Mama and Papa both. And they don't hit. So even though I can't turn around without bumping into someone, even though I'm always tripping over the ladies who come in to sew, even though most of my time I spend inspecting, sorting, and packing bears, even though my parents don't have time anymore for me, my sister, my brother, even though the guys in the neighborhood act different with me now, I guess I'm still lucky.

But I miss the old times. Every Thursday night I would clean out the shop window. And every Friday morning Papa'd set up the new one. While Brooklyn slept Papa turned the window of Michtom's Novelty Store into a candy fantasy. That's Michtom, rhymes with "victim," which is what Papa was in Russia, where the political bear was always at the throat of the Jews, but is not what he is now. In the Old Country all Michtoms were victims but here in Brooklyn we found the land of gold. In Brooklyn we got everything. Well, nearly everything.

Papa, all he has left of his entire family is three sisters. The Queen, Aunt Beast, and Aunt Mouse. That's not their real names. It's just what my sister, Emily, and I call them. The oldest, Aunt Golda, The Queen, she's like a mother to Papa. He would like if she would come to Brooklyn to visit once in a while, but she never does. Papa's sisters, they live on the Lower East Side, in Manhattan, and they don't cross the river. Aunt Beast hates the river. Hates it. Well, I'm not crazy about it, either. No one in our family is. But at least we cross to visit them. The aunts, they never come to see us.

In my opinion Uncle Meyer more than makes up for our lack of visiting Michtom aunts. Uncle Meyer is Mama's brother. Mama pretty much raised Uncle Meyer on her own. Now he lives a seven-minute walk from here, down on Fulton. But he's over at our place all the time.

Uncle Meyer is a free thinker. He, Mama, Papa, they sit around the kitchen table. Yakita, yakita. The world twists its ankle in a pothole, Uncle Meyer calls a meeting. I stick around when Uncle Meyer comes. I keep my mouth shut and my ears open, packing stuffed bears, or cutting mohair, whatever needs doing. I don't even think about slipping away when Uncle Meyer comes. You can learn a lot from grown-ups sitting around a kitchen table. Used to be they spent hours there, but lately we can hardly find the kitchen table. Mama and Papa and their bear business. It's everywhere.

So these days, when Uncle Meyer tells me, "Pull up a chair, Joseph," you bet I do, even if the neighborhood guys are waiting a game for me, which they never used to do and which you'd think would make me happy. Except if they're waiting a game for me and I'm late or I don't show at all, they're angry. They used to just start playing as soon as enough guys showed up on the street. If I made it, great. If I didn't, well, that was okay, too. I liked it better that way. I don't like too much attention on me.

At home I work. I listen. I look. At breakfast, Uncle Meyer drinks Mama's tea, barely letting it cool. I don't know how he does it. He bolts down that scalding tea like a man dying of thirst, then drums his fingers on the empty china. His fingers are like bananas. Not the color. The shape. Long fingers. I look at my hands and hope they finish up like Uncle Meyer's. Papa's hands are okay. But they're small, like lady hands. And they smell like vanilla. I don't want little, sweet-smelling hands like Papa. I want hands that can wrap around a baseball and send it whistling over home plate. Strike-out hands. That's what I want. That's what Uncle Meyer's got.

Uncle Meyer, I don't know why, but he never married. He's younger than Mama but at thirty, he's looking kind of old to me. I don't know. Maybe he's such a free thinker, he thinks marriage would get in his way.

He's not single due to lack of free-thinking females. There's no shortage of them in Brooklyn. In the Michtom house alone we got two, Mama and Emily. Mama. She's the freest thinker I know. She's Papa's princess. Has her way in everything. On the occasions when she and Papa disagree, Mama sends me and Emily out of the room with Benjamin. "Let me have a moment with your father," she'll say. She never yells, she never nags. As the door closes, I hear, "Now, Morris . . ." and then her voice goes a little up, a little down, a little soft, a little warm, and then comes the laughter, "the laughter of Mama's victory," Emily calls it, and when we come back into the kitchen Mama is perched on Papa's lap, her head tucked into his neck, her skirt draped over his legs, and Papa, he is so bewitched by Mama he doesn't know even the day of the week anymore.

No one is immune to Mama. Her thick brown hair, when she lets it loose, curls down her back. Long, soft curls, the color of chocolate. All of us, we do whatever it takes to make Mama happy.

Papa was smart to marry her. That's just one way Papa's smart. In sixteen years he rose from the crowd of penniless greenhorns on the Lower East Side of Manhattan, to independent shopkeeper of Brooklyn, to successful bear manufacturer, to correspondent of presidents. Well, one president. Theodore Roosevelt.

But that's all as much to do with Mama as with Papa. Mama, she's not much for cooking. She's not much by the housekeeping, either, but Mama, most of the time she knows what people want. When the guys say I'm lucky, they can't imagine the half of it. Mama knows what people want and she knows what to do about it.

Sometimes Mama figures it out by accident. That's how it happened, our big break with the bears. Who knew? This past winter, when Mama and Papa sat around the kitchen table reading the paper and saw that cartoon, the one about President Roosevelt refusing to shoot the bear cub in Mississippi, who knew how that one picture would change our lives? Maybe if I'd known I might have hid the paper that day so they never saw it. But I didn't, I didn't know.

Five months ago we were just another family in Brooklyn. Papa sold cigars, candy, writing paper, occasionally a stuffed toy made by Mama. We weren't rich, but we managed. And then they saw the cartoon in the paper.

And that night Mama set the fabric down on the kitchen table. A couple yards of medium-length brown mohair. Papa sketched out roughly what he had in mind and Mama made the pattern: a wide head coming down to a pointed muzzle, round ears, tapered feet. Papa and I did the cutting. Mama did the sewing. Emily, the stuffing. Benjamin, the drooling. We finished two stuffed bears that night, jointed at the arms and legs. Mama stitched thread claws to make the bears look more real. The eyes she designed to resemble Benjamin's. Big and brown. The combination of those eyes and ears, those bears, I guess you could say they looked . . . thoughtful. Who knew "thoughtful" could be so appealing in a stuffed bear?

We should have guessed we were on to something. Benjamin reached his pudgy hands out and did the gimme, gimme with his fingers as Mama sewed up the last stitches on the first bear. She snipped the thread and handed the toy over to Benjamin. That's why she had to make the second bear. Benjamin wouldn't let go of the first.

That was February, five months ago. The moon shone through the shop window. I remember how bright the moon shone as I cleaned out the old display.

And then it was Friday morning. Papa rose earlier than usual, reached into the crib, and slipped the bear out from under Benjamin's arm. Benny whimpered in his sleep but didn't wake. With a bear in each hand, Papa crept downstairs, slipped quietly outside, took the two steps to the shop, and unlocked the door.

It was Brooklyn winter, before dawn. Everything shivered, that's what Papa said. It reminded him of Russia. And thoughts of Russia stirred memories of the Russian bear, symbol of a country that hated its Jews. *That* Russian bear was so different from these innocent things Papa held now under each arm. He was thinking about how his sister Golda, the one Emily and I call The Queen, how Aunt Golda had saved his life by bringing him to America.

Papa leaned the toy bears up against the glass to watch as he prepared the window for them. They were good company, he said, as he arranged a small hill of candy. On top of that hill Papa balanced the first and then the second bear.

We didn't know.

Not even when Benjamin woke crying, sweaty in his crib from all the blankets, his flannel nightgown twisted around him. Benjamin, who never cried. We didn't know.

We ate breakfast together, Mama's usual lumpy oatmeal, before Mr. Kromer started with his clarinet. Before the guys dropped by to pick me up on their way to school and maybe get a free piece of candy. Before Dilly made his first pass with the pickle cart.

Uncle Meyer took the steps two at a time that morning. Banana feet on the end of banana legs, drumming up the stairs.

"We didn't have enough trouble with bears in Russia, Morris?" he asked as he came through the kitchen door in his buffalo coat. "You have to put bears in your shop window?"

Benjamin fussed at Uncle Meyer and Uncle Meyer took the baby from Mama and settled him on his lap. Benjamin patted Uncle Meyer's cold cheeks.

"He must be teething," Papa said.

"Maybe it's teeth," Mama said.

"What's the matter, Benny boy?" Uncle Meyer asked.

Benjamin wrapped his fists around Uncle Meyer's long fingers and cried. Big round tears rolling down his fat cheeks.

"He's not himself this morning," Papa said.

"Why would you make bears, Morris? You escaped the claws of Russia years ago."

"They're not Russian bears, Meyer," Papa said.

"No?"

"No. Go back down," Papa said. "Have a look. They're good bears. They're nice bears. They're Theodore Roosevelt bears. Very American. One-hundred-percent-enlightened bears."

Mama, still in her robe, pushed the newspaper toward her brother with the cartoon that had inspired the stuffed toys in the shop window.

"See," Papa said. "Those bears in the window . . . they're Teddy's bears."

"Teddy's bears, Morris?" Mama said, beaming at Papa. "That's good! Joseph, print what your papa said on a nice piece of card stock. We'll put it in the window with the display."

Benjamin lunged for the newspaper spread in front of Uncle Meyer, nearly tumbling out of Uncle Meyer's lap.

Mama lifted Benny into her arms and studied his face. A trolley rattled past under the window.

"Joseph, take the cartoon before Benjamin ruins it and put that in the window, too," she said. "Arrange everything nice so people can see."

Mama wet a cloth and wiped Benjamin's face. He grabbed the rag and stuck it in his mouth.

"He wants his bear back," Mama said and Emily, looking up from her latest library book, *The Peterkin Papers*, nodded.

"How can he want his bear back?" Papa asked. "How could he even remember he had a bear?"

"He wants the bear, Morris."

"Well, he can't have it," Papa said. "It'll ruin the window to take one out."

"He wants the bear," Mama said.

"He can play with spoons," Papa replied.

"Morris, a moment alone with you please, yes?" Mama asked.

Emily closed her book on her thumb and led the way to the living room. Uncle Meyer carried his scalding tea. I carried Benjamin. Emily, Benjamin, and I sat on the floor, our ears against the closed door.

Benny whimpered around the rag in his mouth while Mama's voice softly rose and fell on the other side of the door.

"Don't worry, Benny," Emily said. "Mama will take care of it. You'll get your bear back."

Uncle Meyer sat on the edge of the sofa, downing his tea. Emily rubbed Benny's back with her hand.

And then came the laughter. Emily nodded. "See," she said.

"Children, Meyer, come," Mama called.

But when we returned to the kitchen, Mama wasn't in Papa's lap. Papa was on his way down the steps. We followed him, a little train of Michtoms with an Uncle Meyer caboose. Mr. Kromer warmed up his clarinet and started a joyful song, a morning nod to the winter streets of Brooklyn.

The store wouldn't open for another ten minutes. It didn't matter. A thick crowd of children bundled in their woolen coats had already gathered in front of the plate glass. They pointed to the mountain of candy. They pointed to the two stuffed bears balanced at its peak.

Our entire family entered the shop. As Papa removed one of the bears from the candy mountain, outside a dozen earnest eyes under caps and hoods followed its path. A dozen disappointed lids blinked as the bear moved toward Benjamin's waiting arms.

Benny's eyes lit up like candles. He dropped the soggy rag and reached out his hands, moving his little fingers in a gimme, gimme.

That was five months ago.

Now, it's Brooklyn summer.

The candy business has dropped off as the bear business has taken over. Every day inside girls fill our flat with bear making. Every day outside girls deliver boxes of finished bears. Papa pays fair and the girls come and go, happy.

Benjamin and his bear are never apart.

Dilly is paying for his kids' bears with pickles.

And Mr. Kromer, his clarinet sasses under the brassy July sun. As the trolleys clang past, a bear sits in the open clarinet case. By noon, most days, that stuffed bear sits on a small hill of coins.